BARREN

Taking of Name

───◆◆───

JON ANTHONY PERROTTI

Version F (feminine pronouns)

Text copyright © 2015 Jon Perrotti

All rights reserved.

ISBN 978-0-9980341-1-9

Cover illustration by Ray Lopez
Book design by Marie Stirk

*Special thanks to my sister Janet
for her tremendous help and encouragement.*

Prologue

The Barren trilogy takes place in a different world from the one we know. It is much like our Earth, and the "uedin" who live there are much like humans, but with some important differences. The uedin populate through asexual reproduction. Much as the female of an Earth species with gender differentiation is known for carrying her eggs from birth, the androgynous uedin carries an embryo, usually singular, for the entirety of its lifespan. The embryo must be born into a very specialized aquatic environment for its first stages of development, and like an amphibian, later metamorphoses into its land-dwelling body. The uedin have evolved to maintain their life-cycle by migrating back and forth between a specific lake which provides the perfect conditions for the aquatic phase and a specific permanent settlement where they carry on a complex society largely unthreatened by predators or competing populations. The adult uedin, at the end of her lifespan, makes a solitary migration back to the lake. There, in a manner comparable to some insect species in which males die immediately after the reproductive act, they give birth to what is essentially a genetic clone, albeit with frequent mutations, and promptly die. Their bodies decompose on the shore of the lake, providing its water with minerals and compounds that nourish the tadpole-like "wetuedin".

The planet has an intermittent wobble in its revolution around its sun that corrects itself every nine years. The result is a repeating nine-year climatic cycle. At the end of each nine-year period, or "novade", a tremendous monsoon occurs. These monsoons bring about substantial flooding, and it is then that the "wetuedin" exit the lake in streams formed by the flooding and migrate salmon-like back to the permanent settlement of the uedin, known to them as "the capital." There they are cared for in special pools until they complete their final transition into land-dwelling uedin. Because a new generation of "wetuedin" arrives at the end of every novade, time is measured in "generations." Child-uedin who have emerged from the special pools are "first generation uedin." Many uedin live to be over a hundred years old, which makes them "twelfth generation."

The species with which the uedin share a symbiotic relationship is a very large stationary being which is highly sentient, but as an organism is physically simple, resembling what one might imagine as a vast underground fungus. It is so evolved in intelligence that it can tune into activity taking place at distances far removed from its own incidental subterranean position. It is able to obtain sustenance by converting the rock and moisture around it at a molecular level into whatever it needs, and its physical body, having lost nearly all vestigial remnants of whatever it was in earlier stages of its evolution, now consists almost entirely of neural matter.

The symbiotic relationship between the uedin and the stationary being has been in place since they both reached levels of intelligence that resulted in an imperative for psychological health. The uedin neither struggle for survival nor face predators, and as a by-product of their androgynous nature and the absence of any innate mating competition, they are inclined toward neither warfare amongst themselves nor power struggle. This would leave them in a quagmire of their own isolation and consequent neurosis, and they would not be able to flourish without some object of attention which could provide them a sense of purpose. The stationary being, likewise, having very little with which to concern itself but a great and burdensome intelligence, requires a focus to make its existence bearable. The stationary being has been able to maintain some mental balance by interacting with the uedin. It interacts by letting its presence be known to them in a very subtle and limited way through telepathy. The uedin respond with adoring attention which the stationary organism is quite able to perceive. However, because of the profound mental sensitivity of the stationary being, it is highly vulnerable to disturbance, and must regularly withdraw from interaction for the sake of its own delicate equilibrium.

Uedin society has two classes: *masters* and *servers*. However, these names do not signify that one class is subservient to the other. Rather, they have different communal functions. The "masters" are those who dictate and manage the operations of "the capital," while the "servers" give their primary attention to a tradition of ritual dedicated to the stationary being, whom the uedin have referred to by various names throughout their history, the current name in use being "Lern Beyana."

The permanent settlement or "capital" is built on a plain through which run numerous dry streams that flow with water during the rainy seasons and carry "wetuedin" during the great monsoon. A propagated forest and agricultural lands lie west of the capital. The region to the east contains cliffs and rock formations, gradually turning into desert. The uedin avoid any suggestion of travel to the lake where they are born, considering that trip to be a sacred one limited to those who are going there to give birth and die. Neither do they have any notion where the stationary being resides; they are satisfied to regard "Lern Beyana" as a vulnerable deity.

The story follows one uedin from childhood and through the course of her life which encompasses the duration of great changes to the entire uedin society and their relationship with their beloved Lern.

Author's note:

The uedin race is one of androgynous humanoid beings who procreate asexually through parthenogenesis; they do not have gender at all. In using English to write about them, a challenge arises with regard to the use of pronouns. Neither "he" nor "she" is really suitable to represent the characters, but English doesn't have gender-neutral pronouns that can be used naturally and inconspicuously. In this, "Version F," the pronouns *she* and *her* were used to provide representations of the uedin and the mythical vadime, while capitalized *She* and *Her* were used to refer to Lern Beyana. An identical "Version M" is available in which the uedin are represented with masculine pronouns. To understand the story as intended, please try to imagine uedin society as one with neither male nor female identification.

BOOK 1

TAKING OF NAME

Part 1

LAST UNNAMED DAYS

Night Road Back to the Capital

A CHILD-UEDIN RAN WITH LIGHT steps toward the capital while the last yellow rays of twilight faded into shadow. The path was littered here and there with rocks that had tumbled down from the slopes over time. The child had run the East Road back and forth for four nights in a row. She knew where the rocks were and skipped around them, hardly looking down. She timed these excursions by shadows and light. She could run out past the capital gate into the slopes and do a few recitations of the Names or a simple shifting exercise and return to Quarterhouse before curfew if she was mindful of the sun and the shadows.

Just off the road, a naked figure, large-boned but weakened and gaunt with starvation, was sitting at the side of a boulder and hunching over, crudely trying to rub thorns from her bare feet. She heard the skipping and raised her head to peer out from the dark. *What was that?* Her head jiggled unsteadily. It sounded like a child-uedin had just passed. She tried to focus. *Where is this? What road was this?* It kept happening— she would try all day to walk toward the southeastern desert, but somehow by night she found herself again just outside the capital wall. She did not want to enter the capital again. There was no help there. Nor would she get any help from the ro-masters whose droning she could hear down in the canyon. If she could just reach the southeastern desert, the sun and heat would bring this to an end. That was all she hoped for now. She dug with stiff and clumsy fingers at the thorns embedded in her bleeding soles, then gave up and leaned back against the rock. She squeezed her eyes shut and waited for some moisture to come into her eyelids. They burned with dryness and dust. A groan escaped her lips. She slowly lowered herself down and lay with her face against the warm ground. She would sleep. In the morning she would be able to tell from the angle of the rising sun where to walk, and she would try again.

The child, entirely unaware of what she had just run past, was all caught up looking at the emerging starscape. The greater moon was in waning to near darkness, and the stars were coming out all at once. The insect song was much less out here on the slopes. She stopped for a moment to listen to the incredible quiet—something she rarely experienced at Quarterhouse. Then she heard the faint singing of ro-uedin. Four of them were singing in deep watery tones somewhere in the canyon just within hearing.

She recognized the voice of one of her tutors, Master Domas, working among the harmonies. They were singing on their way to Haka Cliffs, a favorite sanctuary of the older-generation teaching masters. The ro were elder uedin. They always moved as though they had to tell each foot to step, and spoke as though their minds were gone ahead many days and were disconcerted to have to come back to respond to the present. Some of them, like Master Domas, still did teaching, but most of them wore wise and puzzling expressions and regarded the unnamed child-uedin with dumb wonder. Naturally, most of the unnamed went to the younger masters if they ever had any questions or needs. Master Domas didn't seem quite as old as the others, and it didn't seem fitting that she should be retiring so early to the role of ro-uedin. But the master had been working with her students so diligently in preparation for the Namesgiving that she probably needed a night outside the capital.

The Namesgiving was only a few days away. The child-uedin had noticed that she, along with all the unnamed, found it harder and harder not to slip into singularity. It did not make her happy. Already she was observing differences among the unnamed and perceiving them as "others." Her mind was working differently from theirs. She saw that the generation was ripe for their Namesgiving, and understood the need for its coming. But, for whatever reason, she did not share any of the sense of glory that was built up around the event. She felt a vague distaste for the whole affair, inevitable as it might be. The other child-uedin were so eager for a name, she thought, so they can start asserting themselves. How vulgar!

She caught herself—such a thought was itself too namely. *Just by thinking they are vulgar*, she pondered, *I am riding thoughts of singularity and nameliness.* This kind of inner self-talk was a troubling symptom of growing up, and it seemed only to be getting worse. In lessons, when an unnamed brought up questions or comments that suggested thinking and then thinking about those thoughts and so on, the masters would admonish them to 'stop spiraling.' This child had taken to repeating the command to herself whenever she saw that her mental weaving was going this way.

"Stop spiraling!" she spoke out loud.

The scuffle of her running footsteps broke out of rhythm as she leapt to catch her footing on flat rocks and kicked off the bank in a narrow section. She came to the place where the slopes flattened out into an open field, and the night sky appeared in all its expanse above her. She could see the Broom constellation over the capital. She thought of a famous verse.

> *So happy the bones*
> *There in the sweet pool*
> *White under the stars*
> *And singing, singing.*

Master Domas, whose favorite subject in verse was the Ceulan Lake and the passing-of-life, had taught this verse to the unnamed very early in their schooling. The bones were the bones of uedin gone to the Lake. They sang of their happiness for having completed their passing. A uedin experiences the Lake of Ceulan only twice—once at birth and once at death.

These are beyond the recall or vision of any uedin, but the Lake was everywhere in uedin literature.

If no one ever saw the Lake before her passing, how, the child-uedin wondered, have the poets been able for so many generations to describe it? She wanted to ask Master Domas, but she knew the master wouldn't be good for questioning until after the Namesgiving. She would ask one of the younger masters, even though she knew their answer would be simplified and patronizing.

She was out of the hills, nearing the capital, and the road was straight and clear of debris. She picked up her pace and sprinted up to and through the capital's eastern gate.

Back in the canyon, four ro-uedin masters had switched from the earlier anthem to a droning in deep sustained tones. They stood in a small circle in the black shadow of the canyon wall. No torch was lit and the moonless sky offered little light, but the steam of their breath hitting the cold canyon air still made a visible rising haze above their heads. Domas felt such a splendid relief to be nearing the end of her responsibilities as a Quarterhouse tutor. The generation about to take name was the last one she would ever have to teach. She knew she was really too young to start preparing for her passing, but it was all she could think about—the sweet sleep of Ceulan. In fact her early retirement meant that she would be putting in more years in the ro community than the other masters. She would likely end up getting some high rank, having to be spokesperson, preside over ro-uedin affairs, and essentially be deprived of the freedom of retirement. Even so, she was happy to be done with teaching.

The darkness of the canyon was soothing. Her voice easily found a place in the harmony of the ros' droning. She closed her eyes and let them relax. This kind of droning was usually done by servers, and mostly inside the temple walls. They usually did it to draw the attention and simultaneously soothe Lern Beyana. But sometimes masters practiced the drones to focus themselves, and to draw clarity and sobriety for an important task. Domas and these other ro-masters from the Quarterhouse needed to be mentally focused for the Namesgiving, only a few days away.

Some of the other masters had been fretting earlier that the child-uedin were less competent than previous generations—unprepared, undisciplined. Domas had been around long enough to know that all manner of rumors and complaints returned as each generation approached Namesgiving. It would be fine. It would go well. It would be the same as it had always been.

She let the thoughts dissolve and settled trance-like into the monotone, resolved to a mere humming, diminishing now so that the sound of one could hardly be heard by the next of the four.

Unnamed Talk at Quarterhouse

Just as one of the caretakers sounded curfew with mallet and clapboard, the little unnamed who had been out beyond the eastern gate raced past her and toward the Quarterhouse dormitory. She paused outside to catch her breath. She could hear the rustle and murmur of activity and whispered discussions inside. Lately this commotion had become common. Everyone was full of anticipation for the Namesgiving. The noise was really quite subdued, but to the child-uedin just returned from the quiet of the canyon slopes, it sounded like irreverent clatter and hubbub. She couldn't help feeling a little disgusted. She knew that Namesgiving was one of the most important ceremonies in the capital, but she grasped for negative things to think about it. The Namesgiving was not particularly beautiful, and it featured hardly any homage to Lern Beyana. It was bound to be boring, with the announcements of names going *on and on and on …* !

The truth was that she didn't share the others' excitement about receiving name. She had notions of becoming a great server, and in her mind a server would never relish the taking of name. A server would barely have any self-identity at all—

instead, every aspect of her personality would be forfeited in service to Lern Beyana. This was how to be truly great!

They all want names, she thought to herself, *just so they can make their names great and fat. They're so stupid! Lern Beyana could never be coaxed into giving Her attention to such ignorant little wet ones. Names, names, names … what a lot of nonsense. Lern Beyana doesn't care about their stupid names.*

She had just been out doing an exercise in the canyon and now her mind was messy again by thinking about the taking of name and all the activity ahead. She sighed heavily. The one good thing about taking name was that after she left Quarterhouse she wouldn't have to run back before curfew. She could stay out on the slopes all night and do shifting exercises and recitations.

The main building of Quarterhouse was a long structure with huge exposed beams carved in a pattern simpler and bolder than the more delicate style of newer architecture in the capital. The doorway was hung with a woven tarp suspended from a wooden arm. She pulled the heavy tarp aside, walked in and stepped up onto the polished wooden floor. Here where absolute discipline was ordinarily maintained, tonight there was scurry and fuss. Compared to other domiciles, Quarterhouse was usually a dimly lit place. It had a sweeping roof and awnings that stretched a good length out from the walls on all sides. For this reason, little sunlight passed through the windows. Night or day, it was a rather dark and quiet building. Even so, it had stood for nearly forty generations and was remembered with reverence by the many uedin who claimed it as their childhood abode. Quarterhouse was known for producing great scholars, mostly masters. Scrolls hung on the walls featuring nostalgic verses that had been written about Quarterhouse by poets it had produced.

Tonight it had an uncustomary amount of light. The child-uedin sat in small groups around lamps. The caretaker masters, who stayed with them at night, must have decided to suspend the rules so that they might practice their songs and verses for Namesgiving. A few were going over a tribute song they were planning to sing in honor of ro-masters for whom this would be the last Namesgiving before they left for their passing-of-life. The child-uedin with bird eyes was among the ones practicing. Till lately, only child-uedin with exceptional characteristics could be differentiated one from another. Now as they approached the age of name, physical uniqueness was beginning to show up in their development. After receiving name and taking an assignment in the capital, it would be little time before they would all gradually develop different faces and voices just like their tutors and caretakers. With no names for the years of childhood up until the Namesgiving, there had never been any need to identify individual child-uedin. All praise and correction was given with the intention that it be received without personal implication. Now they were nearing the age of name, and there was an awkward sense of premature self-consciousness. They sometimes referred among themselves to some of the unique ones in simple descriptive terms. There was "bird eyes," and "funny voice." But childhood was not a time of having name or being known at all, and such nicknames were discouraged.

Some of the child-uedin were sitting in a circle quizzing each other on the dates of famous events in the old calendars. A couple of them looked up and gave a salutary nod to the one who had come in from the front hall and was taking her bedding from the closet. She gave a suggestion of a nod back without looking up and stepped around their circle toward a shadowy corner.

She looked as if she were about to put out her bedding already. One of the child-uedin from the circle stood and approached her.

"Do you need space for bedding already?"

"Pretty soon. But go ahead with the quizzing—it's fine."

"Would you like to join?"

"Oh, no thank you."

The questioner regarded the newcomer with curiosity. "Have you just come back from an outside exercise?"

The other looked for the first time into the face of her questioner. There was nothing to see. That one, like herself, had no outstanding characteristics yet. Gazes fixed for a moment, faces like mirror images. "Yes, this one is back from an exercise," she affirmed.

The other smiled with approval. "You will be sharp for the Namesgiving."

"Exercises are not just for the Namesgiving, you know." She immediately regretted saying it. She would be asked to explain and drawn into a discussion.

"Oh, not for the Namesgiving—then for what?"

How could she get out of this? "For ... for ..." She was uncomfortable. Did she know herself the purpose for exercises? For perfection of the self, she supposed. But all the masters had taught, and she knew well that the pursuit of perfection was vain folly. She couldn't say that it was to get the attention of Lern Beyana—such an idea would be considered very inappropriate for a child-uedin.

"This one just happens to like the exercises." It was the truth, though she had never thought about it until just that instant as she heard herself say the words.

"The child-uedin *likes* the exercises." The other child raised her brow in wonder. But she did not tease. She was impressed. "After the Namesgiving, since you'll have a name and all, this one would like very much to know your name, and who you are. This one will have a name too. Both could know the other's name. Would you be willing to do that?"

She was finished unfolding and laying out her matting. She didn't particularly want any friends other than "bird-eyes," who never said anything, but only shared food and games with her. Anyhow, it felt shameful to consider such things prematurely.

"You will have many names to learn after the Namesgiving. Mine will most likely be among them."

"But when this one learns your name, the name will not indicate that you like exercises," she argued.

"Oh, that's right." The child-uedin, with a bored expression, continued to prepare her bedding. She was flattered by this attention, and since it appeared that her aloofness was winning her esteem, she behaved as though she were too tired from her hike back to the capital and didn't want to bother with any of this.

The other child-uedin was not fooled. "Is snobbery part of your exercise?"

This comment could not be ignored. She decided to accept this other child's interest in her. "How would one remember or recognize you to tell a name, even after getting it?"

The other child thought about the problem for a moment. Neither of the them had any noticeable characteristics. They, along with the majority, were quite indistinguishable.

The one who had initiated the discussion got an idea. "Meet me five days after the Namesgiving at the cold well. Then both can know the other's name! And maybe we can go out to the slopes for an exercise!"

It was good that this child proposed an exercise instead of a game of rope-kick or verse contest.

"All right then. This one will meet you at the cold well—five days after Namesgiving, right after morning meal."

"At the cold well." It was agreed. The other child smiled happily and then turned and left her alone to sleep in her corner.

She was soon on her stomach on the thick woven matting. She was beginning to get used to sleeping face down, adult style. Child-uedin usually slept curled up or on their backs. As they grew and matured, they were taught to sleep face down so as not to put pressure on their developing skullwombs. "Our lives bear meaning by the lives we bear" was an adage every uedin heard thousands of times before her own passing.

The child-uedin reached up behind her head to touch the firm, smooth shape of her skullwomb. It was about as big as her hand. Once, one of the masters had pointed out to her that the skullwomb is generally always about the same size as one's outstretched hand. It did not bulge out too greatly, but the crease around it had become more defined in the past year. She was full of wonder about her skullwomb, and the noble task of carrying a life. Master Domas said it a lot: "One's skullwomb is one's crown; to carry it and its precious content is one's highest honor." Here she was, still a child-uedin herself, yet to be named, and even so there was already the beginnings of a tiny life there within, resting dormant beneath the protection of the bony case. It filled her with awe.

She fell asleep listening to some of the others practicing their verses. She could only hear bits and pieces of the memorized lines.

"… 'The grainhouses of Murro shudder in the whitewind, but have not failed for seventy generations' …"

"… I think it's one hundred generations."

"… Quarterhouse text says seventy…"

"… they say you can tell by the carvings on the grainhouses …"

"… Master Domas said one hundred."

Half in slumber, the child-uedin mumbled, not caring that no one would hear her, "… built a hundred generations ago, failed once after thirty..." Then she began to drift into sleep. Images flickered in her mind, of splashing water, then of stately adult uedin in colorful robes, and then of a beautiful, mature uedin kneeling in the shallows of a lakeshore, a golden light emanating from the back of her head. As she bowed forward, putting her head all the way down to the water, the glow grew warmer and brighter, until there was nothing but a delicious golden light that consumed everything, and the last trace of consciousness melted into sweet and restful sleep.

Four Ro-uedin Returning from Haka Cliffs

Uedin history told of times when the land surrounding the capital had been dotted with communities, but most of the outvillages had long since been abandoned. The vast majority of uedin lived within the capital walls, built to concentrate activity as well as protect from eroding winds and scavenging animals. From most places in the capital, one could hear the call of a server singing the morning greeting to Lern Beyana from the tower of the central temple compound.

Master Benar was already awake, preparing boiled grains for the unnamed, when she heard the greeting. She hunched in her cold-weather overrobe, stirring a large kettle. Benar had been a caretaker of the unnamed at Quarterhouse for five generations. She hummed absent-mindedly, completely ignoring the sound of the server's greeting to Lern Beyana. She was thinking about how her duties might change in the next year. If enough of the new generation chose assignments at Quarterhouse, she might be able to dump some of her caretaker duties on the younger masters. She never envied the teaching masters—she was quite satisfied being a caretaker—but she was

TAKING OF NAME

feeling a little bored with it lately. She wanted to do something with adult uedin—something that would give her a chance to gossip and laugh once in a while! The unnamed were nothing but predictable, and she rarely had reason to venture to other parts of the capital. Maybe she could take over the supply duties next novade. Then at least she might get to meet with the distributor masters and do some haggling.

Uedin life followed a nine-year cycle. A novade began with the Great Rains and the flooding of Lake Ceulan. That was when the drystream turned into a raging river that carried down a new generation of wetuedin. The second and third years had rainy seasons as well, but far less rain, and the rain diminished through the subsequent years of the novade. The first year or so was when the caretakers provided for the needs of the wetuedin, then watched their development as they came out of the water. In subsequent years they tended the child-uedin until it was time for them to take name. The Namesgiving was held during the eighth year of a novade. By then there was no rainy season at all. The unnamed were mostly familiar with a dry and baked world. Older generations of uedin knew what was coming, and they projected their anticipation. The sense that something was coming nearer to its completion was heavy in the air.

The Namesgiving was a solemn affair, because with every name came an identity and a destiny. A whole generation of child-uedin were, in one day, given name and brought into the full responsibility of uedin social code. The anonymity of childhood afforded great freedom, but once named, a uedin embarked on her own singular journey toward greatness or mediocrity, dignity or embarrassment. Masters who had worked closely with the unnamed, especially the older ro-masters, often took the opportunity to withdraw from their duties early to engage in retreats before the momentous occasion. Through droning and meditational exercises, they would sharpen and redirect their personal focus from the unnamed back to themselves and Lern Beyana. In this way they detached from the unnamed, setting them free to choose their own names and destinies. Also it was to reorient themselves for a new, soon-to-arrive generation, or in the case of certain ro-uedin, for the long awaited passing-of-life.

When the server sang greeting from the temple that morning, four ro-uedin on their way back to the capital stopped in their tracks to listen. They looked at each other and smiled. Their minds were quieted from the night's exercises, but they easily resumed their normal attitudes and were comfortable with a conversational exchange. There was a moment of waiting to see who would speak first, as each cajoled the other with her eyes to open the discourse.

At the moment the greeting had sounded, they had all recognized the voice. Having lived and studied together for so many generations, the ro masters of Quarterhouse were completely predictable to one another. Sometimes they even unconsciously mouthed the words being said by others as they spoke, so sure were they of the one another's commentary. There were many times when they could just as easily let an entire matter go unsaid, but they were Quarterhouse masters and enjoyed these exchanges.

It was Lemeh who spoke up, a frail-looking ro-uedin with wrinkles around her lips. "Is it Faro?" she asked, as if guessing.

"Yes it's Faro. I recognize her voice." This predictable exchange took place every morning when they heard the server sing greeting.

"Yes, Faro has a fine voice, even at her age."

"She's one of our generation, isn't she?" They all knew she was.

"Remember, elder uedin, I am one generation your junior," said Domas. Of course the other three remembered; this was what they wanted her to say.

"That's right Domas. You are a generation our junior," said Hera.

"Yes, Domas, you are younger, aren't you?" said Lemeh.

"Yes, I am one generation younger."

"Domas is one gen younger. We are all ten novades, but Domas is only nine," confirmed Lemeh with satisfaction.

"Domas, do you recognize Server Faro's voice?"

"Yes, Master Lemeh, I recognize it."

"Even though she is not one of your generation?" asked Hera.

"Yes, Master Hera. Even though she is not of my generation, I recognize Server Faro's voice."

"And what do you think of Server Faro's voice, Master Domas?"

"I think it is a fine voice," responded Domas with a smile. All the elderly ro-uedin smiled together, sharing this pleasant agreement.

"A fine voice, even at ten novades," said Master Hera, and they all nodded approvingly.

"We masters who busy ourselves about the capital and study the codes cannot compare our understanding with those who choose to learn the rituals and be called 'server.'" The other ro-uedin mumbled and nodded their agreement.

"It is the mystery of having name. We all do different things," said Lemeh.

"Yes, we all do different things, don't we?"

"Indeed we do. It is the mystery of having name," Domas affirmed. She enjoyed being with these older ro-uedin and taking part in this kind of predictable discussion, even though it was exactly what the younger masters made fun of.

"But some things we do the same, don't we." said Master Udow with an expression of great importance.

"Oh yes, oh yes, quite right."

"We all do different things, but some things we do the same. You're quite right, Master Udow."

"Good point, Master Udow." They all looked around at each other to make sure they were all in agreement on this point.

Next they waited to see who would say something about the dawn sky, each considering whether she should be the one to speak of it. Now that they had opened up conversation, it was time for someone to comment on the dawn sky, which happened to be pink. Once it was spoken of, it would be easy to play out the chain of responses.

Hera took her turn. "The sky is pink this morning. Isn't there a reference to a pink sky somewhere in the codes?"

"There's a riddle poem," said Domas, "attributed to the ancient High Server Yemel." Though all the masters knew this, Domas had established a name for knowing the codes early on in her training. Now they found comfort in letting her provide the answers as she had always done. She quoted the poem.

> *"A new fish to feed, feed or be fed on*
> *A new Lern to find, feed or be fed on*
> *A pink sky to tell, tell or be told on."*

"Curious, isn't it?" said Lemeh.

"Yes it is a curious riddle," said Hera.

"How curious," agreed Udow.

"What does it mean Master Domas?" said Lemeh.

"Yes, tell us Master Domas," said Hera.

"I only know what the commentary says," said Domas. "Most of the codes say that by 'new fish,' Yemel was referring to the new generation of wetuedin."

"Oh yes, that makes sense, doesn't it," said Hera.

"New fish to feed—the new generation of wetuedin. Yes indeed."

"And the 'new Lern to find,' well that's not so easy. Of course there's only one Lern."

"Oh yes, yes of course. There's only one Lern and that's Lern Beyana," said Hera gravely.

"So it might be a metaphor for having to approach Lern Beyana with fresh honesty and newness every day," continued Domas.

"That must be it!" said Lemeh enthusiastically. They all nodded.

"But what about the pink sky, Master Domas?" asked Udow.

"Yes, Master Domas," said Hera, "What about the pink sky?"

Domas was touched by the sweetness of these elder ro masters. They reminded her in many ways of child-uedin in the early years of their education. "I must apologize for my ignorance, elder masters," she said sincerely. "I don't know what the codes say about the pink sky."

Master Lemeh gave her a very sympathetic look and said, "Oh Master Domas, don't worry about that at all. I'm sure there's no commentary in the codes saying anything at all about the pink sky in Yemel's riddle."

"Oh yes," agreed Hera. "It is, after all, a riddle."

"Very true," said Udow. "It's a riddle and none of the codes has a word to say about the pink sky, or else Master Domas would certainly know what it said, wouldn't she?"

The elder ro-uedin masters all agreed that if there were any conjecture in the codes about the pink sky in Yemel's riddle poem, Master Domas would certainly know what it was.

"I do know one more thing about Yemel," offered Domas.

"Tell us what you know, Master Domas," said Hera encouragingly.

"Yes, Master Domas, do tell us!" said Lemeh.

"The server poet Yemel matured very quickly into her ro period. She retired in her sixth novade and had a very early final pilgrimage. In her ecstatic days before her departure, she communicated only with quotations of poetry."

"How interesting!" said Lemeh. "Her sixth novade—how young she was!"

"I wonder which of us will be the first to be touched by the ecstatic calling."

"Once we've had Namesgiving, it will be less than a year before the new generation arrives. Imagine—if we're all still here, we'll be in our eleventh novade!"

"But not Master Domas!" said Udow with great emphasis.

"Oh no, not Master Domas. Master Domas will only be in her tenth—isn't that right Master Domas?"

"Yes that's right," said Domas, "And most likely I will still be here to greet the new generation."

"As for me," said Hera, "Whether I am gone on my final pilgrimage or remaining in the capital with Master Domas, my heart will be happy either way."

"As for me," said Udow, "I would be gladder, I think, to find the cool waters of Ceulan and let younger generations greet younger generations." She looked around to see if the other masters enjoyed the cleverness of her wording. They nodded with appreciation.

"You've worked hard at your duties as a tutor, Master Udow," said Lemeh.

"It has been difficult," said Udow. "Teaching the unnamed their first of verses and codes has always been the pleasure of our earliers, but they never had to worry before about the child-uedins' *health*."

This reference to the health issues of the unnamed was an unfortunate bumble. Udow had touched on a bitter subject. This broke the comfortable predictability of their discussion. Udow had done this before, and the masters found it hard to be patient with her. The other ro-uedin were immediately aggravated and withheld any response. To enter into a discussion of the barren syndrome on the day before the Namesgiving would bring about a dismal mood and might even be inauspicious.

Incidences of barren uedin could be found occasionally in the history codes, but these were rare and insignificant. In some of the older and more primitive references, when there was an incidence of a child-uedin dying, it was mentioned as a footnote that the child had been barren. It reflected a time when the embryo in a uedin's skullwomb was considered much more important than her own life, and the tragedy of a child-uedin dying without maturing to eventually have passing-of-life was ameliorated by saying that the child was barren *anyway*. Only in recent times had uedin appeared who were actually barren and lived to adulthood, in every case falling into a state of mental and physical depravity before leaving the capital to wander and die in the wilderness. There was a serious concern that barren syndrome was occurring more frequently with each new generation.

Domas wanted very much to find a forum for this taboo subject. But today, she knew, was not the proper time, and perhaps these ro-uedin were not the ones to speak to. This year, for the first time, the masters council had decided that the young uedin were going to be examined after the Namesgiving to determine which ones were barren. To some degree she was relieved that her responsibilities as a Quarterhouse master would, for all intents and purposes, come to an end when the child-uedin were named, but she also felt a grievous concern for them, and she wanted to have a voice in the decision-making to come.

Master Udow, painfully aware that she had brought up an inappropriate topic, fumbled for words, but didn't know what to say.

Hera came to the rescue. "Whether I am gone on my final pilgrimage or still remaining in the capital when the Great Rains come, I'll be happy either way," she said with a self-satisfaction and smug authority that only comes with years of teaching. "Now let's recite the names of the Lern. Master Udow, will you lead?"

"Very good idea Master Hera, and I'd be most happy to lead," said Udow thankfully, and she began the chanting of names.

"Lehera Beyana yana ya ..." It was a chant of all the names found in the codes and records attributed to the Lern. All the ro-uedin would echo after every name.

"Lehera Beyana yana ya …"
"Lerna Beyana ulrana uedina …"
"Lerna Beyana ulrana uedina …"

Domas was glad to enter into the recitation. She was grateful for the company of these fellow ro-uedin. Their company was as consoling during these retreats as the meditation itself.

"Lern Beyan kiman kiman uedin olorrr …"
"Lern Beyan kiman kiman uedin olorrr …"

Names-Eve Observances Interrupted

The day before the Namesgiving ceremony was reserved for final lectures and rehearsals. The activities of the day were held on the grounds of Quarterhouse, which had the oldest and largest facilities. Unnamed came from other domiciles around the capital as well as a few from an outvillage. They congregated in clusters around the main building of Quarterhouse until the masters gave signals for Names-Eve Observances to begin. The unnamed then filed around the heavy-roofed building, down a long earth ramp, and through a grove of greenbark trees to a great clearing where they formed a large circle. There were over four hundred of them from the various domiciles. This was, however, considered a small generation.

The Namesgiving itself, of course, would be held in the main plaza in front of the central temple with nearly every uedin in the capital in attendance. The activities of Names-Eve, on the other hand, were an insider tradition of the domicile masters. It was not a "ceremony" and therefore didn't belong to the servers. The masters claimed it as their own and regarded it with much sentimental ado.

"Unnamed, be mindful!" The child-uedin all responded to the command in slow precision as they were trained, sinking and placing their feet behind them until they came down to their knees. Then they simultaneously lifted their arms in a uniform gesture to suggest straightening their overrobes, punctuating their readiness and attention.

In unison they called out a salute, *"LERN BEYANA, ULRAN UEDINA!"*

A teaching master from one of the other domiciles was giving the Names-Eve address. She rose, strode to the center of the circle, and projected her voice.

"Unnamed! All of this child-generation have lived until today in simplicity! All have studied, played, and slept in common! None have yet been visited by blame nor by praise! The studies of one have earned her no reward; likewise the fool and the cheater have suffered no consequences!" The master turned as she spoke, addressing every part of the circle. Now she paused and gave them a chance to comprehend what she was saying. The majority of them were Quarterhouse unnamed; to them, the face of any adult uedin outside of their own tutors and caretakers seemed strange and foreign. Her speech and inflections even sounded peculiar to them. The content of her speech was the same thing they had been hearing from their own masters for hundreds of days. They were more interested in the novelty of her appearance and voice.

"Names will bring destinies to all uedin! Good work will follow the name of the uedin who worked! Good poem will follow

the name of the uedin who spoke it! But also ill and error will follow the name of the uedin who does them! One uedin will prefer the sound of her own name to the name of Lern Beyana! Another will despise the sound of her own name and hide always from having name! Strive always to be like neither of these, but to own and understand the name that one receives!"

The child-uedin remained still in their seated position. This was not like one of the masters' lessons; there could be no nodding or questioning here. This short speech would be the only one the youths would hear during the Namesgiving events. Tomorrow's actual ceremony would include no speeches, only ritual and the taking of names.

The child-uedin who had gone on exercise the day before and fallen asleep wondering over her own skullwomb sat in the circle, identical in appearance with her fellow unnamed. Like the rest of the other Quarterhouse unnamed, she was listening for the first time to the words of a master from outside. However, she did manage to derive more from the speech than many of her peers. " … *to own and understand the name that is given one* …"

Some of the unnamed had been whispering about the idea of there being a connection between name and destiny. The notion was prevalent in uedin mythology, but the masters were unenthusiastic when questioned about whether there was any truth to it. They were more comfortable with codes, history, and verse than notions about such esoteric matters. If nothing else, to "own and understand the name that is given one" must at least be a way of saying to accept one's place and live honorably. Such thoughts made that child-uedin reconsider her discomfort about the pending Namesgiving. Perhaps she had been underestimating the importance of taking name. Distracted by these thoughts, she failed to hear the announcement being made by one of the Quarterhouse tutors, Master Udow. Master Udow was a very kind and gentle master, but she moved so slowly and rarely said anything of importance. The child-uedin had not been listening, and didn't hear what Master Udow said when there came a sudden murmuring in the circle and craning of necks. Something interesting had happened.

"What was that?" She tapped the child-uedin beside her. "What did Master Udow say?"

"Some servers are coming!" said the other one.

"Servers? To the Names-Eve events?"

"Sshhh!"

Two individuals wearing undyed and undecorated wrappings that conformed to their arms and legs—quite unlike the masters' stately robes—appeared with a large, shallow bowl. None of the child-uedin had ever seen servers before. They certainly did look different from the masters. They were thin and lithesome, with a physical quality that suggested youthfulness and age at the same time. Servers would be overseeing the Namesgiving ceremonies the next day, but none of the unnamed had expected to see a server at Names-Eve.

Udow spoke in her slow and gentle manner. "The servers, who honor us with their visit, are going to show us how to take part in the smoke purification ritual." She slowed down unnecessarily when she used the word "purification." She always spoke to the unnamed as if they were still three years old. They knew about sourembers—coals made from burning the roots of a shrub that grew in the canyon. The incense emitted was an intoxicant used in Beyanic ritual.

She continued. "Today we are only *practicing* the movement—there are no sourembers." She used exaggerated expression on her face to communicate this twist to the unnamed, as if they might not understand without her nonverbal cues. "Tomorrow, it will be *real* sourember smoke!" She paused to let them all understand, as if it were a difficult thing to grasp. "And it's *very important* that you receive *just enough* smoke to prepare you for drawing your name blocks, but *not too much*—or it could make you sick, and that would be an awful thing to happen at the Namesgiving, wouldn't it?" The unnamed couldn't help wondering why she needed to talk so slowly. "So we all need to pay *very close attention* as our guests demonstrate for us." Udow gestured thanks to the servers and hobbled back among the other waiting masters.

Without speaking, the servers stepped forth and began to demonstrate how sourember smoke was received. One of them sat in the same style as the unnamed so that they would understand that they were expected to do as she was doing. The other carried one of the bowls past her in very slow but unyielding movement. The server in the seated position lifted her hand in perfect timing to scoop some of the imaginary smoke and draw it gracefully to her nose. The movement she made with her hands was reminiscent of the uedin gesture often used to show humble gratitude.

After repeating the demonstration so that everyone in the circle could see clearly, the servers began their way around to let the unnamed practice the movement. This time, rather than just carrying the sourember vessel, the servers alternated, carrying it and passing it to one another in continuous movements. It was always necessary to take turns carrying the sourembers and keep moving because the carriers could be easily overwhelmed by the fumes. The child-uedin lifted their hands as the vessel passed by and waved the imaginary smoke toward themselves as they had been shown. Some of them were corrected because their movements were sloppy or hastily paced.

When the servers had finished going over the smoke purification, Udow was stepping forth to say more when the program was interrupted by some commotion coming through the greenbark trees.

A figure stepped out, dressed in wrappings like the other servers. The unnamed thought that it was another server who had come to assist in the demonstrations. But something was wrong. For one thing, this was a ro-uedin, a very old one—probably just as old as any of the ro-masters at Quarterhouse. It didn't make sense that she would be coming to Names-Eve to demonstrate with the other younger servers. Her wrappings were loose and disheveled, and her eyes had a wild look in them. The younger servers immediately started running to her side, but before they reached her, she began to shout.

"*Great trouble comes with this generation! Lern Beyana withdraws! She cannot bear to see uedin life turn inside out!*" The two servers who had demonstrated the smoke purification ritual reached the ro-server and tried to calm her.

"*The Lake does not know what it sends us!*" cried the old server. "*The bones of our earliers would crumble in sorrow if they knew what they send us!*"

The younger servers were now physically holding and trying to pacify her. The old uedin did not fight them but kept on ranting.

"*... feed or be fed on, feed or be fed on ...*" she moaned.

They locked arms around the ro-uedin and led her away. She began sobbing, but went with them without struggle. The child-uedin all had their heads down in feigned unawareness as they had been trained to do when a disturbance arose for which their attention provided no help, like when a caretaker spilled something or another unnamed was being admonished.

Udow had been on the verge of announcing the next event when the commotion had begun. All the masters were observing from outside the circle. Their procession would come later in the program. Hera, Lemeh, and Domas were standing right behind Udow. Udow turned and looked at them with distress. How should she carry on after such an interruption?

"Shall I say something to the unnamed?" asked Domas.

"Oh, please do, Master Domas!" said Udow with urgency.

Domas stepped forward. What could she say? By now some of the child-uedin were whispering to one another about what the old server had said.

"Unnamed, listen!" she shouted, and the circle of child-uedin immediately was quiet.

"You've learned that every uedin goes into ecstasy when the instincts for final pilgrimage replace normal sensibilities." She was a ro-uedin herself, but spoke with composure and authority. "It's unfortunate that our Names-Eve observances were interrupted just now, but when you leave your domiciles and take residence in various assignments around the capital, you will get used to witnessing ro-uedin coming into their ecstasy. Many of your masters, including myself, are near the time of our passing, and you may see them say and do things that are not consistent with how we are taught." Domas was doing her best to put fears and concerns to rest. "When that happens, we must not be frightened. The server we just heard was expressing her own fears—it is something that happens when a ro-uedin enters her ecstasy—but it must be understood in its proper perspective. We don't have to worry. Not for ourselves, and not for the ro-uedin. Even while she expresses her fears, she is preparing for her final pilgrimage to Ceulan. She has to purge her bad dreams; to do otherwise would be to hold on to the burning pan. It is her time for passing-of-life, and it is a time of great glory and fulfillment that every uedin lives for. Let us be centered now for the sake of Lern Beyana who sustains us. *Lern Beyana, Ulran Uedina!*"

"*LERN BEYANA ULRAN UEDINA!*" the unnamed called out in response.

"Now we will commence with our Names-Eve activities," said Domas, and stepped back among the other masters.

Udow put her hand on Domas's shoulder and spoke in her ear. "Oh, Master Domas," she said with sincerity, "You are a credit to Quarterhouse—to the whole capital." Hera and Lemeh nodded.

"Well, I think I may need some reassurance myself about Server Faro's raving." They had all recognized Faro's voice immediately. She had called the morning greeting just hours earlier. With an exchange of glances they agreed to discuss the matter at a later time. For now they needed to concern themselves with getting through the Names-Eve activities.

The unnamed were expecting to hear a review of the Leafsap ritual, which would be part of the Namesgiving. And they expected another run-through of the formations and procedure for the receiving of name. But the servers, who were supposed to perform the Leafsap, had exited with the ro-uedin. The schedule was running behind, so those parts of the rehearsal were omitted. They would go right into the teaching masters' procession. The teaching masters quickly gathered at the base of the earth ramp and reorganized themselves. The unnamed stood and parted for them to walk to the center of the field.

It was an old tradition of Namesgiving for the teaching masters to test the unnamed by quizzing them publicly on the codes and calling on them for songs and famous poems.

During the Namesgiving itself, this was carried out as a formality. To avoid any awkwardness or embarrassment, nothing challenging would be asked of the unnamed during the ceremony. The Names-Eve, on the other hand, was a real chance for the child-uedin to show their knowledge and win praise for their whole generation. Masters and unnamed alike looked forward to the Names-Eve quizzing.

Old Master Hera was the first to pose a question to the youths. She squinted and tried to look menacing, but she was too kindly in her ro-uedin manner to intimidate. "What did the early High Server Rewo of the Generation of the Clay Bridge write in her diary about failed novades?"

Bashful smiles could be seen on the faces of the child-uedin. This was an easy one. Failed novades were rare in uedin history, and happened only when rain was not sufficient to flood the Lake of Ceulan and fill the drystream. Rewo's comments had set a precedent for the common uedin belief. Master Hera shuffled out from the place where the teaching masters were standing in the center, and tapped an unnamed on top of the head to hear her response.

The child-uedin slowly delivered the memorized response, "Rewo wrote in her diary that she was sad to be deprived of the pleasures of raising one generation lost, but she believed that their short and innocent lives as wetuedin would not be displeasing to Lern Beyana."

"Correct!" shouted Master Hera gleefully. She nodded the next turn to her friend Master Domas.

Domas's question was more obscure.

"There was one outvillager from the generations during the Scattering who is remembered for her poems of labor. Name the poet and recite the poem she wrote about harvesting the fieldpears."

The first child-uedin Domas called on knelt and rubbed her face to show that she humbly acknowledged her ignorance. Domas then chose the child-uedin right next to her.

"The poet was Galbi," she replied, "and the fieldpear poem is but two lines:

Creaking baskets complain, and tired fingers beg
How can fieldpears taste better than leisure in the shade?"

"You recalled the poem well," said Master Domas, "But the first line is the other way around. It's 'Tired fingers beg and creaking baskets complain.'"

The child touched her folded hands to smiling lips in a gesture of gratitude for the correction. Domas smiled in return. As uneasy a fate as this generation may face, she felt for them a fierce love and pride she sometimes forgot she was capable of. They were equal, she was sure, to their trials to come.

Master Benar Ponders Recent Events

The unnamed fasted and kept silence until the opening of the Namesgiving. Tonight there was no activity at Quarterhouse, but lamps were lit where some of the child-uedin sat writing poems to commemorate their last night of namelessness.

Master Benar had finished writing a rudimentary account of the day's events in the caretakers' log. It was one of the many small responsibilities she had taken up during her years as caretaker. Benar preferred doing small tasks to the scholarly pursuits and grand theories of the teaching masters. The unnamed would have been surprised to learn that she had once been expertly versed in the codes, but the masters knew it. She had chosen to spend her days helping in the upkeep of the Quarterhouse, planning suppers and supervising chores.

She was sitting at her favorite spot near the ovens in the kitchen house. She had a little table and stool there where she often read in privacy or wrote out her schedules. It was also there that she sometimes wrote the mundane notes of the caretakers' log. Usually it was simple notations about repairs and supplies, with the occasional student accident or illness. It was not anything that the teaching masters would bother with.

Benar finished writing a short entry into the log, then got up and put it back on its shelf and looked around for something to eat. Fortunately the masters did not have to fast along with the child-uedin for the Namesgiving. She had lived through enough generations of Namesgivings that it felt not too terribly unlike any other night to her. She would be more interested after the Namesgiving was past. That was when the child-uedin developed with startling swiftness, during their ninth year when they were newly-named, the majority taking assignments in other parts of the capital and preparing to leave Quarterhouse. Benar herself had somehow defaulted on that matter and remained at the domicile. She neither regretted nor felt great pride in having stayed to become a Quarterhouse master.

She checked the crock of sweetbulbs that she was pickling. They looked and smelled delicious. She had privately spied a small patch of sweetbulb plants growing out of place among the bean bushes about ten days ago. They were probably freak remnants of a crop that was cultivated there during the last novade. They were the bluest bulbs she had seen in years, sure to be especially sweet. She wondered if they were ready to eat. The liquor in which they pickled had turned blue. She drew one of the bulbs out with a little spear, put it on a small dish and returned to her table to eat.

Pity it was too small a batch to share with the unnamed. As she bit off one clove at a time, she listened to the silence of Quarterhouse. At present many of them were probably writing their final rhymes for the unnamed collection. It was a compilation of simple rhymes written by generations of child-uedin. Traditionally the uedin refrained from claiming them after receiving name, and so an area of study had grown up around the speculation about what rhymes were written by what great uedin.

Quiet would be the character of Quarterhouse for the next year. The ninth year was always quiet as the newly-named moved on to apprenticeships.

Benar thought of this generation and their performance at the day's program. They had behaved appropriately in the face of the disturbance. All she bothered to write in the log was that the Names-Eve activities had been taken place as scheduled, with a minor upset from an ecstatic ro-server who must have followed the two younger servers demonstrating the smoke purification. She added that caretakers from all the domiciles had brought provisions to feed their own unnamed after the program, and that she had sampled the nutmeal biscuits from Whiteroof, and that they were very good but probably tasted better when warm. No need to go into detail in the caretakers' log. If anything that happened during the Names-Eve activities required more precise record keeping, the teaching masters would handle it. Fortunately that old ro-server had only disturbed the Names-Eve activities, and not the Namesgiving itself.

There had been a time when Benar looked at the inevitability of ecstasy, pilgrimage, and passing-of-life with great longing. The masters taught the unnamed that the final ecstasy was the natural crescendo of emotion regarding the passing-of-life that followed a lifetime of gradual preparation. From what Benar had seen, real ecstatic behavior was not nearly so pleasant. It appeared as sudden mental deterioration and transition to animal instincts. Benar was raised at Quarterhouse and, having chosen to join the masters there, had never left. First she watched her own tutors and caretakers go through their ecstasy and departure, followed in time by many senior masters she worked with. It was simply a fact of life. Still, there was power to the myth of a glorious passing, and no one could know what the experience was really like until it was that uedin's time. Perhaps that's why it was disturbing to see the ro-server appearing so tormented in what was supposed to be a wonderful condition. She did not envy the teaching masters who faced greater challenges to explain and make sense of uedin life for each new generation of unnamed. Life was not nearly as simple as it had been when she was growing up. Now there was this awful predicament, with many uedin turning out to be barren. Two novades ago, long before Benar had taken over as head caretaker of Quarterhouse, a tutor who came from her own generation had developed symptoms and soon after disappeared. It was then that word began to circulate around the capital that that particular generation had a high incidence of barren syndrome. Then in the following novade, an even larger number of third-generation uedin displayed symptoms of barren syndrome. They knew then that it was not any particular generation that was manifesting it—it was simply on the increase, and it revealed itself when the affected individuals were into their second to third novade.

It was becoming difficult to tend the unnamed without wondering who among them were the unlucky ones. Now an examination was being considered. What would be the result if it was soon determined who the barren were, well before they even showed symptoms? Well, it would not be her problem to solve! She felt a bit of guilty relief, knowing that these questions were the burdens of other masters.

She chewed and swallowed the last bit of sweetbulb and rinsed her dish. She got the idea of surprising Master Hera with a jar of the sweetbulbs before retiring. She lifted the lamp to fetch a jar from the storage closet.

Domas Discusses Faro's Ecstasy with Colleagues

Hera poured hot tea into cups for herself and her guests. Master Gisef, a teaching master of her same generation, had stopped to wish her a happy Namesgiving, and shortly afterwards two of her companions from the previous night's retreat at the Haka Cliffs—Master Domas and Master Lemeh—came to talk about the Names-Eve ceremony.

Master Lemeh was upset about the incident with the ro-server who had interrupted the program. "She was uttering lines from the same poem Master Domas quoted earlier yesterday morning on the way back from our exercise." She shook her head with concern in a very ro manner. "Didn't you hear her, Master Domas?"

"Yes, I did. She said a few lines from the same one of Yemel's riddle poems that we'd been talking about. That was strange."

"How could Faro have known?"

"Well, I'm sure it was just coincidence," said Domas. "Remember that pink sky on the morning before Names-Eve—it probably reminded a lot of uedin around the capital of Yemel's poem."

"As the younger servers were taking her away, I heard her say 'The bones at the Lake cry out in despair'—that is not the sort of thing that comes from ecstasy," said Lemeh with frustration. But the other masters did not seem to share her concern.

"Of course it's simple ecstasy," said Gisef coolly, "What do you think the ecstasy is but dementia?"

Master Hera pursed her lips and set the cups on the table a little more noisily than necessary. She was slightly annoyed with Gisef. Hera had been Gisef's mentor for many years. Gisef's research had helped to determine the location of the ruins of an ancient farming compound—an abandoned outvillage that had completely slipped into oblivion. Hera was never jealous or spiteful about the fact that the junior master she had trained had gone on to outperform her. But Gisef was too opinionated, and too self-assured—*that* was what irritated Hera.

Domas was a little more polite. "Master Lemeh," she said, "I think you may be reading too much into this. It was extraordinary that Server Faro was singing greeting in the morning and had entered into the ecstasy by afternoon, but we shouldn't let our imaginations run away with us."

Hera contributed, "Also, Master Lemeh, we know that any bones or remains that collect at Ceulan Lake are just bones. After the passing-of-life, there isn't any life left in them."

"Very true, Master Hera, very true. There is no life left in the bones after passing-of-life," said Lemeh. "Server Faro was speaking in metaphor—but I do think it was some sort of … prophecy."

"Prophecy?" Gisef smirked. "Master Lemeh, you sound like you're starting to rave yourself."

"What do you think Server Faro might have been prophesying, Master Lemeh?" asked Domas patiently.

"I don't know," said Lemeh, "But the servers know things we don't know."

"The servers themselves do not believe in prophecy," said Gisef dismissively. "You know the tenets. Remember? 'Lern Beyana does not speak.'"

"Master Lemeh, maybe it would be best for us to put this out of our minds for the time being." said Hera. "Let's not lose the benefit of last night's retreat. Tomorrow is the Namesgiving. Our dear unnamed will soon be leaving us—don't we want our minds to be clear and fresh when they take their names?"

Lemeh was glad to put the topic aside, at least until Master Gisef left. "Regardless of all that," she said, "I'm sure we all agree that Master Domas did a fine job of smoothing things over after the servers took Faro away." They were all ready to join in a chorus of praise for Domas when lamplight broke across the shadows by the door. It was Benar.

"Forgive me for interrupting you, masters," said Benar, "I brought this jar of sweetbulbs to Master Hera, you can all share it of course …"

"Why, that was very kind of you Master Benar." said Hera. "We were just about to retire, but maybe we'll have one with another cup of tea. Would you care to join us?"

"No thank you Master Hera. I'm going to check in on the unnamed in the dormitory before retiring myself," said Benar, "But I must tell you what I witnessed on my way over here. I thought I heard some singing coming from over by the eastern gate, so I walked over to see what it was. There was a group of servers canting a farewell. Server Faro was departing the capital. I waited and spoke to one of the younger servers. According to her, Server Faro was granted emergency departure for her final pilgrimage tonight."

"You see Master Lemeh? Server Faro was ecstatic," said Gisef. "Nothing more."

"Strange, though, for them to send her off without announcement the night before Namesgiving." said Domas thoughtfully.

"Yes," said Benar, "the servers must have considered it an emergency."

"Dementia," said Gisef, opening the jar to smell the pickles.

Master Lemeh stared momentarily into Benar's lantern light. She didn't want to discuss Faro anymore.

"Well that's about all. Good night, masters. Rest well tonight for tomorrow's Namesgiving."

"Good night, Master Benar," said Hera. "And thank you for the sweetbulbs."

Namesgiving Ceremonies

The morning of the Namesgiving was overcast. There would be no signs of rain for many moon cycles to come; on the contrary, the region was extremely dry. The gray sky was the result of dust.

The capital plaza was in temple jurisdiction. Servers oversaw all ceremonies there, and there were never any speeches or announcements. Uedin poured in from every direction, but observed silence when they entered the space. The unnamed sat without movement in their positions. Four servers entered the central space to do a shifting exercise. They removed their wrappings to allow freer movement. Without a word of introduction they sprang into position and began the shifting.

Shifting was one of three exercise traditions. The others were droning and mind-stilling. All uedin knew how to do the exercises, but the servers developed them to extraordinary levels. To the masters, seeing the servers do a shifting was a reminder that servers pursued an entirely different path—one that made them seem foreign even while they lived within the same capital walls.

They maneuvered through series of strenuous poses, held in muscle-splitting tension, and showed no trace of stress or effort on their faces. The child-uedin, sitting erectly, watched in awe. Each time the servers took a form it was held and intensified for a prolonged period. At its most intense moment, the force of the position wrenched the servers' muscles so that they slid into knots under their skin, and the bones of their arms and legs could be seen bowing into curves. No hint of anything but calm was seen on the servers' faces. Then in a sweeping motion the servers swung themselves and locked into the next position. The power escalated with each vaulting shift, until the servers worked to the famed 'flat form.' In this, the most difficult of the shifting poses, they conformed their bodies to the flatness of the ground. The successful executor of this pose was supposed to be able to dislocate her joints and spread her muscles so that only her skullwomb would edge above the flattened plane of her body. These servers were young, but their skill was stunning. Three notes were hummed, marking the end of the exercise. The servers slowly drew back into their normal body frames. The child-uedin could now sit back on their feet as the shifters methodically rewrapped themselves.

Throngs of uedin stood around the periphery of the expansive temple plaza and on the long and sleek arc of steps cut into stone that stretched toward the temple's main entrance. The crowd presented a confetti of turquoise and white, the colors of master and server ceremonial vestment with the occasional capital guard master standing out in her green guard's robe. In the center of the plaza the unnamed knelt at attention for the exercises, positioned in a perfect circle. They were spaced considerably apart from one another, signifying their new singularity; though always part of the whole, they would never again be anonymous or free of self.

The higher-ranking servers watched in critical scrutiny as the younger servers prepared the sourembers for the smoke purification. For the sourembers to have any effect, the root had to be moldy. It did not light easily. It took skill to get the sourembers going just enough to provide a fine incense without burning up too quickly, which was even more of a concern in dry weather. The scent crept quickly over the entire plaza. Uedin both loved and revered the sourember smoke. A faint whiff of it could be pleasantly sweet at a distance, but when servers carried the urn of burning sourember past, it was nearly overpowering. As it passed by, each unnamed extended one arm forth and drew a wave of smoke toward her face. The rivulets of rising purplish gray smoke were immediately intoxicating. With increased sensitivity, the unnamed became aware of the sensation of the warm wind blowing against their faces. They felt the pressure of their knees and feet against the stone surface they knelt on. They heard the rustle of the crowd who stood around them observing, and felt the weight of their own shoulders and heads. Certainly, the effect of the sourembers was ideal for the Namesgiving, since it was awakening them to an acute sense of *self*—the self that is at once powerful and helpless.

A high-ranking server began to sing. She was starting the Leafsap ritual. It was one of the oldest and most primitive of uedin rituals, with little known of its origins. The ancient-tongued utterances were not completely understood by even the servers who practiced and recited them in ritual. It was a crude and primitive performance compared to any other uedin ritual, and nowhere in the singing or movement was there any reference to Lern Beyana. Translations had been attempted. There was a part that talked about mice stealing food, saying that those mice must be caught and killed. Another part of the song supposedly said that anyone who relieves herself in an unfitting place and fouls the water will be denied water thereafter. The unnamed always laughed when this was reviewed by one of the teaching masters. The words of the Leafsap were unimportant. What was strange about the Leafsap ritual was the unique emphasis on the uedin themselves. It was bawdy and primitive, harkening back to an age when uedin lived in innocent self-centeredness. The chanter's voice grew guttural and raucous, and a single representative uedin strode forth unclad and proceeded in an earthy dance of bold and deliberately crude movement, bouncing with the yells of the server. A chorus of other voices joined the cantor achieving a practiced dissonance. The dancer's movement was deliberately arrogant and jerky. At various points she spat and yelled and comically wiggled her head on her neck. The reverent atmosphere of the plaza gave way to a mischievous mood. Masters laughed and called out to the clown, responding in fun to her exaggerated movement. When she leapt forth they playfully gasped and withdrew. When she yelled and made a *baaa* sound like a goat, they pretended to be afraid and playfully shrieked in fear. The unnamed were still in their seated positions, but they laughed and clapped with delight. At the culmination of the dance, a server pulled out a decorated wagon in which was propped a gnarled shrub, dug up from the roots. It was only about as tall as an adult uedin but had a fat, bulbous trunk with spongy, cork-like bark. Its branches bore few leaves, those being thick, heavy, and deep green. A few young servers drew the wagon along the circle, and as it passed, some of the unnamed took needles from their sleeves and stuck them easily into the soft bark. After this, the tree was wheeled to the center where the dancer then did a strange thing. She reached up and started to pluck leaves from the tree. The fat, heavy leaves broke right off. From them leaked a white fluid. The server dancing the dance now boldly smeared the tree "blood" in stripes on her own naked chest and face. The servers' chorus of discordant voices were now emitting a kind of coughing, laughing sound, which accentuated the grotesque display. The Leafsap ritual came to its conclusion when the tree was stripped of its very last leaf. When the server picked it, the chorus broke into a completely different type of song, something much more akin to the usual harmonies of Beyanic droning. The server brought the last leaf of the tree to her face, put it in her mouth, chewed it and swallowed. Then she stretched her arms in pantomime-like movements and lay on the ground beside the cart as if she were going to sleep. Two servers lifted her effortlessly and placed her with the now bare tree and drew them away. The crowd applauded and cheered.

The teaching masters took their positions for the quizzing. The turquoise of their ceremonial garments gave them a brilliant appearance. A young master announced the commencement of the Namesgiving quizzing. The unnamed watched with relief as Master Lemeh stepped forward to ask the first question.

> *"Eight stars decorate my eyes*
> *Shall I throw back my hood for more,*
> *But no, my precious will get lost'*

Poet, period, context." She walked slowly out and touched the head of a child-uedin to solicit the answer.

"The poet is Malta. It was written in the fourth novade after the wheatcrop failure and the fasting years. Malta hides in her verse a commentary on the Council's decision to plow fields outside what was then the accepted territory of the capital and its outvillages."

"And what is her commentary?"

"The eight stars she admires will be lost in the myriad if she looks all around the night sky; likewise, the sanctity of limited uedin fields will be diminished if we venture beyond them to new land. This was her concern."

"Well recalled," asserted Master Lemeh.

Master Olup stepped forward to ask the next question. "Give the history of the Clay Bridge construction." It was a long recitation, but one that each of them had memorized. A child-uedin was chosen for response.

> *"The Clay Bridge was built beyond the south capital gate.*
> *It was built to replace a wooden bridge washed out by the Great Rains.*

The child's voice was timid and high-pitched, and any stirring that had been audible in the crowd until then stopped. Everyone listened to hear this innocent one, a most unlikely focus of the attention of what was practically the entire population of the capital, get through the tale.

> *Master Demip built a bridge like no bridge ever before.*
> *She challenged all the common building wisdom of the day.*
> *She used black clay mixed with cottontree wool.*
> *Black clay is always found under dry streams.*
> *It holds tiny air bubbles and can't be fired.*

The child rattled on with the memorized history in a clumsy little voice. Other unnamed were mouthing the words as they listened.

> "*Many thought that the bridge would fall apart in hard rain.*
> *They ridiculed Demip saying, 'See if it lasts a novade!'*

Nine years later, when the time of Rains came,
the whole capital watched to see how the bridge would fare.
But that novade failed and the Great Rains never came!
The bridge went untested, and no wetuedin arrived!
Oh what grief when this happens to our capital!
Not much attention was given to the fact
that Demip's clay bridge had been spared its challenge.
For nine quiet years with no unnamed,
The clay bridge served all the traffic to the south
even while most considered it to be temporary.
Finally the dry novade came to a close.
No uedin thought or cared more about the bridge.
The capital longed for a new arrival of wetuedin.
What a terrible thing they couldn't have imagined.
The Great Rains alluded the capital again!
Sad were the uedin who lived in that time.
Never before had this thing occurred.
Two lost generations, two failed novades,
How, indeed, did they endure such a time?
In those days uedin were more superstitious.
Some high-ranking servers were suspecting Demip.
Did she use sorcery to stop the Great Rains?
Just to save her reputation and her clay bridge?

Soon there were petitions to have the bridge
    destroyed.
But sensible voices staved off the action
in arguments that went on for the full nine years.
All of those suspicions were finally put to rest
when the Great Rains came hard and stormy
three novades after the bridge's construction.
A plentiful and healthy generation of wetuedin
arrived in the hatching pools, to everyone's relief.
And, as we all know, the bridge stood strong.
The unimagined by-product of these events
started to become clear within a few novades.
The last generation to come before the bridge
had benefited richly during these years
with training and schooling unprecedented,
all time and resources given to them.
So many poets and scholars arose
including great masters as Talid and Rewo
and mystic server Ulie, just to name a few.
The generation gave back every blessing to the
    capital
and came to be known as the Clay Bridge
    Generation
celebrated in history as the greatest ever.
As for Demip's original clay bridge,
it stood eighteen novades and was finally replaced
after it was damaged by land tremor, not rain!

> *A replacement bridge was built of the same clay mix.*
> *It still functions during wet seasons and Great Rains*
> *We can see it just outside the south capital gate."*

"Well recalled," said Master Olup, delighted with the child's success but trying not to smile quite as much as the faces in the crowd lest she make light of the event. The real quizzing had taken place during the rehearsal, and today's questions and answers were predictable to all involved. But there was still a specific pleasure in watching the unnamed rise to the occasion. She couldn't help feeling proud of them. Despite the rumors about this generation's being afflicted, there was every reason to expect greatness from them.

After a few more representative queries had been made to demonstrate the competency of the new generation, the names-taking began. Some younger servers wheeled in two carts bearing the name blocks. Three ro-servers came out and stood between the two carts. They would be the pronouncer of names. Finally, there was yet another server who carried a willow branch. She walked around the circle and randomly stopped before one of the child-uedin and touched her skull-cap with the branch. The child rose and walked to the center of the plaza where the carts rested. She drew a block from the cart facing the east. She held it up and looked at the pronouncers of names. After a moment to consider the options, one of them spoke the syllable in a loud voice: "*Dhe.*" The child then drew from the cart facing the west and held up the character block. The pronouncers read it and nodded to each other. The server pronounced it: "*Gil.*" The child placed both of the blocks on the ground before the carts and rubbed her face in a quick gesture of humility.

Then using the first person reference for the first time, she called out for all to hear: "I am Dhegil."

The crowd called out, "YOU ARE DHEGIL!" acknowledging Dhegil's arrival at selfhood.

Another server smeared the child-uedin's forehead with a bit of red paste to show that she had received name and sent her back to her position in the circle. The server with the willow branch randomly chose another, who practiced the same steps. The pronouncers gave her the syllables "Ra" and "Wep," and she similarly was the first to speak her own name, declaring "I am Rawep," to which the crowd responded, "YOU ARE RAWEP!" With nearly four hundred names to be given, the task would take some hours. But there was genuine excitement as each of the child-uedin received her name.

The child who had not looked forward to receiving name was now just as curious and eager to know what name she would receive as any of the others. She listened as names were pronounced. She was a little ashamed for ever thinking that taking name was unseemly. Now the names seemed beautiful and mysterious.

"Yu."

"Net."

"I am Yunet."

"YOU ARE YUNET!" shouted the crowd.

The next unnamed came forth and drew character blocks from the carts.

"Bel."

"Na."

"I am Belna."

"YOU ARE BELNA!"

This process went on for such a long time that her mind wandered and she grew tired of sitting still, but then suddenly, the server was standing in front of her and touching her head with the willow branch. She stood quickly and approached the cart. The intoxication of the sourember smoke was mostly worn off now, and she regarded the first cartful of syllable blocks with some nervousness. The blocks were marked with ancient characters, many of which were quite different from the letters used in reading and writing the codes and literature at lessons. She drew one block which had a simple character that appealed to her eye and held it up. The pronouncers conferred momentarily. Then one looked up and pronounced: "El." The child-uedin then moved her hand over the other cart. She quickly grabbed the block under her hand without regard to the look of the character inscribed on it. She held it up. The servers looked at it and pronounced it: "Enn." She placed the blocks on the ground, rubbed her face in humility, and called out, "I am Elenn." The crowded shouted back, "YOU ARE

TAKING OF NAME

ELENN!" She felt a strange sense of possibility awaken in her as she heard the name shouted back to her. It *wasn't* all superficiality, she thought. There *is* destiny in name—she could feel it. After getting the mark on her forehead and returning to her place in the circle, she repeated in her mind, "I am Elenn, I am Elenn… "

Quarterhouse Masters' Thoughts and Recollections

Benar heard someone coming and tried to appear distracted with her notes. She was hiding out in the kitchen. The Quarterhouse masters always met on the flatpool observation deck on the day after Namesgiving. That was where the generation first arrived, and now that they were named, it would be no time before their sweet uniform features gave way to individual appearances and personalities. The day after Namesgiving was a day of congratulations and nostalgia for the masters.

Benar, however, didn't want to run into Hera and the rest. It turned out she had not given her sweetbulbs enough time in the brine for their proper pickling, and they had given her a dreadful case of gas on the very day of the ceremony—the worst imaginable time for such a disaster. She was sure that Hera and the other masters had experienced a similar result, thanks to her poor judgment. How embarrassing! Hera herself could be counted on to say nothing about it, but since the cursed pickles had been shared with the others, she was resigned to hear some humiliating commentary sooner or later. Domas might report the side effects with brutal honesty, or she might just as likely forget about them since her mind was always moving on. It was that wild-headed Gisef who was likely to tease most mercilessly.

She fuddled with her caretaker's log, trying to look occupied. Who was coming? She heard Lemeh's voice as the door tarp was pulled aside.

She looked down and turned pages as if searching for some important notation.

"… Oh, yes, Master Domas, 'disturbing'—you're quite right. That's exactly what it was, disturbing." said Lemeh in her drawn out ro-uedin speech.

"I wonder how many of the other masters noticed," said Domas. Benar was careful not to look up, but she imagined they were looking at her.

"Well now," said Lemeh thoughtfully, "I suppose it depends on whether they got a lot of the sourember smoke or not. One may not notice much else if one has gotten a lot of sourember smoke."

"Master Domas, Master Lemeh!" Benar, no longer able to conceal her shame, slapped the book down on the table top and looked up at her tormentors. "Please forgive me for my error—the sweetbulbs …"

"Master Benar!" interrupted Lemeh, "I didn't even see you there. We were just discussing some of the name-character combinations that came up at the Namesgiving ceremony, weren't we Master Domas?"

"We came to get some fresh water. There's a terrible dry wind today," said Domas.

"Name-character combinations?" Benar blinked and looked back and forth at them. She was still adjusting to the fact that they were not talking about her sweetbulbs. She reached for a cup and began to pump water for them.

"Oh yes. Master Domas is so alert!" Lemeh nodded and bulged her eyes as she spoke. "Master Domas noticed quite a few recurrences during yesterday's ceremony—didn't you, Master Domas?"

"There were more than I remember at other Namesgivings," said Domas. She accepted a cup of water.

"What were some of them again, Master Domas?—oh, Master Domas has such a good memory—what were some of them?"

"Well, we have a Rinok, same name as the historian Rinok who wrote about the Scattering, and we have a Dinil—Dinil, of course, was one of the artists who carved the relief sculptures in the Haka Cliffs."

"And you said we have a Pilke," interrupted Lemeh, then whispered the side comment to Benar: "Pilke was a corrupt server." Lemeh, smiling as she took a cup of water from Benar with both hands, seemed to enjoy the fact that there was a server mentioned somewhere in the codes who was known to have been corrupt.

"Well the old name is Pil-*ka* ," corrected Domas, "and the modern reading is 'Tilke', but the characters are the same exactly."

"I hadn't noticed so many recurrences," said Benar. Was there no end, she inwardly asked herself, to the minutiae that the teaching masters loved to pick apart? "But name recurrences aren't really that uncommon, are they?"

"Well, they do occur," responded Domas, "but considering the number of character blocks, the odds of so many recurrences are very small."

"This generation had a lot of smart child-uedin." Benar got an extra cup of water for herself. "Do you suppose a few of them picked out characters for names that they recognized?"

"Oh—I wonder. That would be like cheating!" Lemeh gasped at the thought. "Do you think they might have, Master Domas?"

Domas squinted and drew in a breath of doubt. "I hardly think so. There isn't time to look during the taking of name. Besides, what child-uedin would want the name of Pilka?"

"No, you're right," Lemeh nodded to acknowledge the authority of Domas's pronouncement. "They couldn't have picked them out." She shook her head dismissively. "No child-uedin would want the name of Pilka. She was a corrupt server. No, Master Benar, there couldn't have been anything like that."

Benar made no comment. She wasn't really very interested in this business about name recurrences. She wondered if they were just being polite by not mentioning the pickled sweetbulbs.

"Coincidence would be my guess," said Domas. "And maybe it's best if we say little about it. We wouldn't want them to be unduly influenced by the associations of their names. This 'Tilke' will make her own identity if she's given sufficient chance.

Perhaps she'll bring a new distinction to the name. At any rate, the frequency of recurrences was exceptional."

Benar thought momentarily about her own name, which had never seemed particularly distinguished. It was made from the combined characters of "elbow" and "river silt." She gazed tiredly at Domas's concentrated expression.

"Oh by the way, Benar," said Lemeh suddenly, "thank you for the sweetbulbs. We all enjoyed them very much."

"Yes, tasty," mumbled Domas, and when she said, "Astonishing, really," it was unclear what she was referring to, the sweetbulbs or the recurrence of names. Benar nodded sheepishly and said nothing.

A young master appeared at the door and held up the tarp. "Excuse me, masters," she said, "The other ro-masters are starting a game of shell-toss on the observation deck. They're looking for you, Master Lemeh."

"Oh, I'd better go." Lemeh finished her water and put down her cup. "Master Domas, you're retiring soon—you should learn to play shell-toss with us."

"Go ahead, Master Lemeh, I'll come and join you shortly," said Domas. Lemeh followed the other master out the door. Domas and Benar listened to Lemeh's voice trailing away as she told the younger master that she was the better at shell-toss than any of the other Quarterhouse ro-uedin.

After a pause, Benar said, "Master Lemeh was so stern when I had her as a tutor. I am amazed at the changes that have come over her during this past novade."

"Yes, well I'm finding that one's perspective changes radically when one reaches nine or ten generations," said Domas.

"Master Lemeh will be tenth novade?" asked Benar.

"No, Master Lemeh will be eleventh. I will be tenth." Domas looked at Benar thoughtfully. "And you will be sixth—is that correct, Master Benar?"

"Yes, that's right. I was in the last big generation. Five hundred and eighty."

"Yes, we were incredibly busy with all of you."

"Namegiving went quickly yesterday, didn't it?"

"A small generation," said Domas, "Only four hundred and twelve. It's disastrous how many we're losing to barren syndrome."

"That reminds me," said Benar, "Do you remember the young teaching master who left Quarterhouse with the syndrome a few novades back? I was head caretaker at the time. What was her name?"

"Oh, that was Temil," said Domas. "She was earning a fine reputation—knew botany exceptionally well."

"Temil—that's right. She was a fine young master." said Benar, "I hate to think what happened to her."

"It's unsettling to think of how many unnamed we may have impressed with an elevated notion of passing-of-life who will never themselves experience it. We have sometimes idealized it too much. I have been guilty of doing so myself."

Benar was glad that Domas was willing to discuss the syndrome. "When did it start?" she asked.

"We don't know. Of course we have those references to child-uedin that died, but those child-uedin were never really barren. There are some earlier notations about uedin who went into ecstasy very early and died in the desert. It wasn't understood at that time that they were actually barren."

"Is it true that the council may conduct an examination of the newly-named?"

"We are discussing it. What do you think, Master Benar?"

"If I were a young uedin and there were a chance that I were going to be barren, I would not want to know."

"Nor would I," said Domas. "But the capital is at risk."

Benar looked at Domas's face and saw the lifetime of worry and hard thinking that Domas had given to the capital. Now she was a ro-uedin, and her being on the masters council would probably deprive her of an easy retirement.

"Come on," said Benar. "Let's go out to the observation deck. Master Lemeh wants to teach you how to play shell-toss."

"All right, thank you, Master Benar," Domas patted her shoulder appreciatively as she followed her out. "By the way, Master, you might want to let your sweetbulbs stay in the brine a little longer next time. I only had a few, but I hear Master Gisef ate almost the whole jar and had some unlucky results." She knew Benar was laughing in front of her because of the way she was hunching and her shoulders were jiggling.

Meeting at Cold Well

Tilke walked across the area where she had recently received name, through the plaza in front of the central temple, and started down the stairway to the sunken court of the cold well. She could see the other newly-named one already waiting at the cold well. As their eyes met, the two smiled together in an instant of delight and understanding. Tilke was not shy about revealing her enthusiasm at meeting this pre-name friend. She hopped down the last few stone steps to the cold well.

"Hello, my good friend who likes the exercises!" She spoke, just a bit too loudly, catching her breath. "I am Tilke."

Elenn answered with the line that had been reverberating through her mind since the Namesgiving. "I am Elenn."

"A wonderful name. Very glad to meet you Elenn. I hope you don't mind my interrogating you at Quarterhouse when we talked the other night. I really do think there's something exceptional about a child-uedin who likes the exercises."

"Well, I'm not sure if being exceptional is a good thing," said Elenn, trying to sound very serious, "but thank you for your kindness." She strived perhaps too hard for sincerity.

Tilke laughed. What a peculiar and interesting character this Elenn was, she thought.

Elenn sensed Tilke's natural and unselfconscious ease in her laugh. It was so unnamely. It was wonderful, but it made her feel ashamed. Here was this bright and airy young uedin, acting as a mirror to show her her own self-absorption.

"Would you like some dried peach?" Tilke pulled a small sack of leathery dried peach slices from her pocket. Elenn accepted a couple slices of the fruit and began to chew on it happily. She wanted to be the type of young uedin who chewed happily on dried peach slices, and she was grateful knowing that she had plenty to learn from her new friend.

"Do you still want to do an exercise?" asked Elenn. "We don't have to if you don't want to."

"I do want to. You weren't fibbing about liking the exercises, were you?"

"Well," Elenn started to think about what might be the best answer but then stopped herself and just told the truth, "No, I really do like the exercises … my favorite thing, practically."

Tilke nodded her head toward the direction of the eastern gate. "Then let's go!"

They ascended the stairs from the cold well and trotted past the servers' library. Tilke gave half of the remaining dried peach to Elenn and crammed the rest into her own mouth. Elenn found it strangely delightful to see her do this. It occurred to Elenn that some of the behavior that she had once thought to be unseemly in the other child-uedin might make a completely different impression once the individual had a name and an identity. She pondered the thought and gazed wonderingly at Tilke, who returned a broad smile. Her teeth were yellow from chewing dried peaches.

When they got to the edge of the slopes, Tilke invited Elenn to pick the location and activity for a shared exercise. Elenn chose a dry creek bed with silverweed growing around it. They began by sitting side by side right in the depression of the dried creek bed and humming in a warbling tenor. They were attempting a droning exercise.

"Try to get that buzzing sound," said Elenn. "When more than one uedin does the droning exercise properly, it's supposed to create a buzzing sound. When servers drone, they get such a strong buzzing sound that they can stop droning and the buzz will keep on going."

They tried repeatedly to get the buzzing sound.

"Hhnnnnnnnnnnnnnnnnnnmmmmmmmmmmm…"

"Hhnnnnnnnnnnnnnnnnnnmmmmmmmmmmm…"

"Was that it? Was that the buzzing sound?"

"No, it's got to sound like it's coming from outside of our heads."

"Hhnnnnnnnnnnnnnnnnnnmmmmmmmmmmm…"

"I think I heard once that you have to know how to do circular breathing in order to get the buzzing sound."

"What's circular breathing?"

"You inhale at the same time that you're droning."

"That's impossible!"

"No, it's not! The servers do it all the time when they do droning exercise."

"Hhnnnnnnnnnnnnnnnnnnmmmmmmmmmmm…"

"Hhnnnnnnnnnnnnnnnnnnmmmmmmmmmmmm…"

"Ah—did you hear that?"

"That was not the buzzing sound!"

"Yes it was! I heard it!"

The two newly-named practiced the droning exercise until they started to get headaches. Next they tried some simple shifting exercises. This was easier because of their youthful flexibility. Elenn was thrilled to know another newly-named who was serious and competent at exercises.

Walking home Elenn asked, "Tilke, have you considered joining the servers?"

"I have. But I don't think I will. I think I'll stay in Quarterhouse."

"Stay in the Quarterhouse?" Elenn couldn't imagine such a disappointing choice. "You mean if you became a master you wouldn't even take an assignment outside Quarterhouse?"

"I like Quarterhouse," said Tilke. "And if I stayed at Quarterhouse I could look forward to all the changes of each novade, new generations and all that. Master Hera told me that once you enter the temple you never get to come out and every day is the same."

"Master Hera told you that?"

"Yes. And they make you work hard, too. And their food is very plain."

"But think of it!" said Elenn, "Servers experience what masters never do. They take the exercises to perfection. They reach Lern Beyana."

"You really do like the exercises, don't you."

"Better than all the codes and schedules and busy nonsense of the masters."

"Well, remember what the masters taught us though— '*We all do different things, for it's the mystery of having name.*'"

"That's true," said Elenn quietly. "You're right, Tilke."

"But if you want to be a server, I think you should be one. You'll be Server Elenn! Won't that be fine!"

Elenn didn't answer right away. She had never heard or even thought of the title of server followed by her own name. "That's what I want more than anything else," she said softly. "But I'm not sure I'm suitable. I'm afraid I'm too namely."

"Too namely?! We only received our names five days ago!" laughed Tilke. "Besides, no one will remember your name if you become a server. They never do."

Part 2

NEWLY-NAMED

Outing to the Lichen Fields

Half a year had barely passed since Namesgiving, and the newly-named already looked more like adults than child-ue-din. Those who weren't already apprenticed or committed to appointments in the capital were taking a long hike to the lichen fields. Joined by a few of the younger masters from the capital guards, they walked the Chalk Road on their way to collect the lichen that grew thick and red on the rock hills northwest of the capital during the dry season.

Elenn and Tilke stopped on the path to look at a nest of caterpillars in a shrub. "That kind doesn't make silk," said Tilke. They stood quietly watching the creatures wiggling in their nest. Elenn saw that the rest of the group was getting pretty far ahead of them, but she liked the fact that Tilke didn't rush.

Tilke looked up from the nest finally. "Now that they've hatched, they have to get away from the nest or else they'll get eaten by birds or something." She seemed unconcerned about falling behind. Elenn decided it was time to bring up the topic that had been on her mind.

"Tilke, you know a lot of the newly-named have already chosen assignments. Have you decided what you're going to do?" She hoped at least that Tilke wouldn't still be thinking of staying at Quarterhouse.

Tilke looked away from the caterpillar nest. "Master Leksa told me she thought I might make a good apprentice at the paper mill. I'm not sure yet. How about you?"

Elenn felt her chest tighten with emotion. Nothing had changed for her. "I want to join the servers. I'm thinking about the Beyan temple."

Tilke noticed that Elenn called it the "Beyan temple" instead of the "central temple." That was the servers' own name for their compound. She responded calmly. "Well, I know that's what you've talked about. You should do that Elenn. You'd be very good there, I'm sure."

"I don't know if I would be or not. I've always been one of the first to speak up, the first to raise my voice with questions, or to stand and recite something during the lessons."

"That doesn't matter Elenn. If you become a server, you'll learn to be quiet. You'll learn to listen more. Don't stop yourself from doing what you want to do just because you have some self doubt."

"I'm not saying I'm not going to do it, I'm just saying I'm not sure if I'll be a good server or not."

"What is a good server?" asked Tilke.

Elenn said nothing. She wanted to say, "*You—you* would be a good server." But somehow she knew that Tilke would take that as mere flattery. What Elenn wanted to do was convince Tilke to consider a server assignment because Tilke was so perfect for it. She was so perfect for it that she herself couldn't see it. Her modesty was part of what would make her a perfect server.

"Tilke, why don't you come with me."

"Come with you?"

"Join the servers with me."

"Oh, Elenn, I don't see myself as a server. I think I would fit in much better as a paper-maker. Or if I don't do that, maybe the construction masters …"

"But don't you see? That's exactly why you belong with the servers! You have such an ease about you, Tilke. You'd be satisfied to stir paper pulp every day. You'd probably be satisfied to sit and peel greencones every day for the rest of your life. Do you know how special that is?"

Tilke wasn't really sure if Elenn was serious or making fun of her. "What do you mean by that, Elenn? Do you think I'm not bright?"

"Tilke!" Elenn turned and looked at her with tears in her eyes. "You *are* a server! I know you are! If I have any hope of being a server, then you absolutely have to be one!" Elenn felt a little embarrassed by her outburst, but there was no taking back or denying what she had said, and it was what she truly believed. She took a breath and gazed up at the group walking ahead of them on the Chalk Road. "If you don't become a server, then I don't think I can be one."

Tilke could have said that this was not sensible—that Elenn had to choose her own assignment, and Tilke would choose hers. But she knew that Elenn was beyond that. Elenn may have thought about things too much, but she always pursued what was true at a level that had to be respected. She often heard Elenn say things which could be easily squashed by recalling simple teachings that they had both received from the masters. But she had learned that doing so always left her feeling vaguely empty. Now Elenn was telling her that she, Tilke, *was bound to be* a server—*already*. It scared Tilke.

"Elenn, I don't know what to think about what you're saying. Maybe I should talk to Master Leksa."

"No! You can't talk to Master Leksa about this. Don't you understand? The masters would never encourage anyone to become a server. They only know what it is to be masters—the server world is foreign to them."

"Elenn, I know you would not intentionally steer me wrong. But, I'm sorry, I think you're saying all this because you are afraid to enter the temple alone." Though she said it, it was not really what she thought at all—it just seemed like something that might have been true—if she were talking to anyone else but Elenn. She immediately saw Elenn's disappointment, and she regretted her words.

Elenn could not allow her personal feeling of being misjudged stop her from pursuing her point. She turned away and looked down the road where the other newly-named had now disappeared. "We should hurry. Please do one thing for me. Now, before you have a chance to tell yourself all the reasons why you don't believe me, before you convince yourself that you don't have the heart of a server, will you chant the Names of the Lern with me as we walk?"

There was no acceptable way to refuse this request and, anyhow, Tilke didn't necessarily want to refuse it. What if Elenn was right? If Tilke had the makings of a server, it was not something she needed to resist. She found that she took to the exercises with great ease. But strangely, she felt no interest whatsoever in entering the server community. Anyhow, it would not hurt anything to recite the Names.

Tilke started right in: *"Lehera Beyana Yana Ya."* Her voice was smooth and calm.

Elenn echoed the first line of the Names chant with her own choked and unsteady voice: *"Lehera Beyana yana ya."*

Tilke rattled off the next line with shallow regard. The light carelessness of Tilke's chanting was exactly—Elenn just knew—exactly what would be pleasing to the Lern.

The lichen had grown fat and red in the aridity of the novade's end. It was so abundant that by the time Elenn and Tilke got to the spot where it was being harvested, some of the others in the group had already collected as much as they could carry. It was beautifully thick and spongy. Tilke and Elenn spoke little as they cut soft bands of it from the rocks and filled their sacks. There was plenty to dry for the future, and it would make many pots of wonderful soup.

One of the chaperoning guard masters approached Tilke and Elenn. Tilke knew her. "It's Master Deben. I wonder what she wants." She wasn't very tall. From a distance, her guard's robe was the only thing that distinguished her from the newly-named.

"Lichen is beautiful, isn't it?" She said with a friendly smile. "I forgot what it was like. I took this hike when I was newly-named. The lichen must grow the best in the ninth year. It likes the dry."

Tilke answered. "Yes, it's growing nice and thick right here. And the color! But I don't suppose it will stay this rich in color after it's been dried."

"No," said Deben, "it will change a little bit. But this is the nicest I've ever seen." Elenn looked up and gave a respectful nod.

"The name of the uedin?" asked the master.

Elenn introduced herself self-consciously. "This one is Elenn."

"Elenn, very well. I am Deben. And you … I think we may have met?"

"Yes Master Deben, I am Tilke. I am one of Master Leksa's advisees."

"Ah, yes. We met at Quarterhouse once. Well, Elenn and Tilke, it looks like you've collected quite a bit there. There's a small spring behind that hill. Everyone's going over there to drink water and rest before heading back. Walk over together?"

"Yes, master, thank you," answered Tilke. They picked up their sacks and followed the guard.

"What guard station are you with, Master Deben?" asked Elenn, trying to show a polite interest.

"I'm a second-generation guard in the Flatpools District—close to the Quarterhouse," she said with a bit of reticence. She seemed to know that a guard assignment was not highly favored among the academic-minded Quarterhouse masters. She added, "I was glad to get this chaperoning duty. I always like getting out of the capital when I can."

"Chaperoning duty?" Elenn asked. The guards had accompanied them on outings when they were unnamed, but she didn't understand why it should be necessary now. She had been hiking in the slopes by herself for the past few years.

"There have been some concerns," Deben responded vaguely. "Anyhow I like coming out here. And I do think the lichen is beautiful."

"I've heard that the guards use some of the shifting exercises in their training program." Elenn was trying to show some admiration. Deben gave her an appreciative smile. She knew that Elenn was trying to be kind.

"Well, yes, we practice some of the quicker shifting exercises as part of our physical training. Have you ever attempting any shifting?"

"Elenn is very gifted at shifting." Tilke spoke without hesitating. Elenn was mildly embarrassed, but before she could say a word, Tilke went further. "She wants to be a server. And she wants me to follow her into temple life." Elenn felt her hands unconsciously rise to her face in embarrassment. She almost dropped her sack of lichen. She couldn't believe Tilke had just said what she said.

Deben looked at them both strangely. "Well," she searched for something appropriate to say, "choosing one's place in the capital is not an easy task."

Suddenly they all heard shouting and then a loud whistle coming from the area around the spring. Deben dropped the sack she was carrying and ran ahead. Tilke and Elenn picked up Deben's sack and hurried after her.

When they got to the spring, it was hard to see at first what was causing the commotion. The other guard was ushering the newly-named away from the spring. Deben had run ahead and seemed to be addressing an older uedin on the other side of the crowd.

"What's happening?" asked Tilke.

"I don't know, but I think that uedin is unclothed. I wonder if it's a ro-uedin who's entered her ecstasy."

"No, she's too young. I wonder what she's doing."

The uedin was naked and had a large, hulking frame. She stumbled from behind Deben and took a few awkward steps into the middle of the spring pond. She was holding something. It looked red, and Elenn thought it was a piece of lichen. She reached and drew some of the red material to her mouth.

"That doesn't make sense," said Tilke. "You can't eat lichen until it's been cured." Then they saw what it was. It was the carcass of a small wild dog. Its head had been crushed against rocks. The uedin's eyes darted about and then she looked down at the twisted body of the dead animal in her hands. When she drew her hand up over the dog's crushed head, Elenn thought the uedin was about to stroke it with pity. Instead, with a strange and distracted gaze, she jabbed her fingers into the bloody skull area, scooped out a handful of brains, and ate them. Purplish dog blood covered her mouth and face. They couldn't hear what Deben was saying to her. Whatever it was, she didn't seem to comprehend. She only looked about with a crazed and tormented expression. None of the newly-named had ever witnessed such a horrible scene.

"Shield the Lern! Do you know what that one is, Elenn?" said Tilke in almost a whisper. "It's one of the barren."

Tilke Visits the Paper Mill

"We use oil from springpear seeds to reinforce heavy paper for scroll jackets. It reacts with most of the dyes and turns them brown, which is why we don't do a lot of coloration in this room. Usually the masters add their own ornamentation on scroll jackets in the copy house." Tilke was getting some introductory exposure to paper-making operations, thanks to an appointment made for her by Master Leksa. It seemed like a very deliberate and clean activity. Tilke was thinking it would be a very suitable way to spend her life.

The master giving her the orientation, a Quarterhouse uedin by the name of Karam, was probably two novades her senior. She had a calm and patient air that appealed greatly to Tilke. "See how the springpear seeds have to be shelled and ground there? That's the kind of menial task you would probably have to settle for during the early part of your apprenticeship. It could be a while before you get to actually work with the mash and screens. It takes a certain individual to thrive on this kind of work. Do you think this is something that would interest you?"

"Master Leksa suggested I consider this assignment. I think she probably has a very good sense about me."

"Well, you know," said the master in a lower tone, "it's not what anyone would call an exciting assignment." The change in her voice suggested that she was being especially candid. "I had difficulty for the first few years. I had considered so many options—weather scouting, the vinegar brewery … then, after I settled on the paper mill, for a long time all I could think of was what a mistake I had made—how any other work would have been more satisfying." Tilke was touched by her honesty. The master continued, "But gradually I came to love this work. The masters who work here don't need to discuss anything. We know the process, and we know each other so completely that we work together in silence. Sometimes days will pass with no words, only a smile or a nod here and there."

Tilke listened with appreciation. She looked at the samples hanging on the walls. "And the paper itself is beautiful," Tilke offered. "It seems a shame that it all goes on to get marked with ink."

The master smiled. "You're thinking like a papermaker already. Some are fond of saying that the best poetry is found on un-inked paper, with nothing on it but the grain and texture of the mash."

"I can imagine learning to have that kind of appreciation," said Tilke.

"Well, young uedin, if you choose to bring your name to the paper mill, I'm sure we will all be very happy to welcome you."

"Thank you, master, for your kind encouragement," answered Tilke. But she was not sure yet where she would submit her name. Elenn was right when she warned her that neither Master Leksa, nor any other master, would openly encourage a newly-named uedin to consider serverhood. Tilke didn't understand exactly how any newly-named ever chose to be a server. The temple made little attempt to recruit. In her case, it hadn't been any kind of serious consideration until Elenn had pressed her with the idea. How nice it would be if the servers provided some kind of orientation to life in the temple like she was getting at the paper mill, but there was never anything like that.

"I'm going to check the charcoal burners in the drying room," said Karam. "Please stay and observe as much as you like. If you have questions, you can ask any of us." She departed with a relaxed hand-to-face gesture. Tilke walked to the next chamber where a few old ro-uedin were shredding dried huskroot with slow and graceful movement. Everything about the paper mill appealed to her—the unassuming character of the masters, the quiet industry of the operation, and the subtle beauty of the product. It did not appear to be a very challenging assignment. Yet maybe there would be times when the tedium of the work would be a challenge in itself, as apparently it once had been for Master Karam.

Tilke wasn't sure if challenge was something she personally needed or not. But now, even as she saw a perfectly suitable option for her assignment, she could not stop thinking about the challenge that Elenn had presented.

Where was Elenn anyhow? Two days after the outing to the lichen fields, Elenn had sought her out to tell her what she had heard. The barren uedin that they had seen had been taken into custody and was in the infirmary. The medics had sedated her and were doing some kind of tests on her. Master Domas was on the council now, and she had apparently gotten involved—that's how Elenn had heard about it. Elenn had found Tilke, told her just that, and left. They had hardly had a chance to talk, and Elenn was off to research something. That had been two days ago, and Tilke hadn't seen her since.

Maybe Elenn was offended because Tilke had blurted out to that guard master that Elenn wanted to become a server and wanted Tilke to follow. Tilke knew that the guard master was the last uedin Elenn would have opened up to, and maybe that's why Tilke had the need to just say it—to test the idea by speaking it aloud to an outsider. Tilke didn't like secrets.

She reached up and ran her fingers over the grain of a paper sample. It was appealing to the touch. Here was something beautiful, but anchored in utility. The other life, the life of the server, had no such concrete assurance. It was a life of giving attention to the timid Lern Beyana, who could only endure the softest regard, Lern Beyana who sustained them all but had to be wooed into accepting their devotion. Elenn was asking her to consider such a life. It was a challenge that seemed utterly beyond her, even to the point of absurdity.

A Horrible Realization

Two days after the hike to the lichen fields, Elenn received permission to go to the capital libraries. The masters at the entrance directed her to the temple archives collection with no questions. The interior of the main building was paneled with an iridescent saltstone that allowed visibility with little lamplight. For some reason, it attracted small birds who got trapped inside. There always seemed to be a few stray ones flitting about in the corridors.

Most of the newly-named were involved in formal inquiries, and some were already starting their apprenticeships, but all were dispersed around the capital, and there were no more classes at Quarterhouse or any of the domiciles. The library was relatively quiet. The main hall seemed empty. A few masters were researching their own pet interests, and some newly-named were, for the same reason as Elenn, doing independent investigations relating to their possible assignments.

Elenn received directions and found her way around the maze of rooms to the collection of temple verses and documents. Servers produced little manuscript. She had come to the library in hopes of finding something written by servers in the past who had struggled with nameliness. But once she started looking, Elenn found that she was fascinated by *anything* written by servers, and she began to browse randomly. There were delicate little booklets containing short poems. There were a few compilations of tributes and commentaries in which pages written on odd, unmatching paper were bound together. It was something Elenn had never seen in any of the masters' literature. There was a large, crumbling set of miscellaneous writings jacketed in featherwood bark. Elenn pulled one of the volumes down. She opened it up and saw that it contained hand-written transcription, apparently by uedin who had little calligraphy training. The writing was simple and innocent-looking. She read a poem.

> *Orange vineberries for our tea.*
> *Kitchen sweep dust for our tea.*
> *Rumbling thunder for our tea.*
> *Tongue and closed eyes for our tea.*

These were interesting indeed. Elenn continued pouring over them until a particular one caught her eye. She recognized a line. It was a poem from a high server named Yemel. She had never heard of Yemel before.

> *A new fish to feed, feed or be fed on*
> *A new Lern to find, feed or be fed on*
> *A pink sky to tell, tell or be told on.*

She recognized a line from somewhere. Then it came to her—at the Names-Eve program the ecstatic ro-uedin who had been crying about the Lern kept saying "feed or be fed on." She looked around to see if there was a collection of Yemel's works, but there were no completed works of any uedin in the server collection. Servers apparently did not produce such tribute publications. There was a footnote, however. It indicated that the fish poem came from Yemel's journals. Maybe the journals had been preserved or copied for the collections.

Elenn began scouring the shelves for any sign of Yemel's journals. She finally found one thin text marked with the single character *Ye*. She opened it and looked at the first page. There was the name, Yemel. It was too small to be a journal that had been kept for any significant period of time. Perhaps it was all that had survived. Elenn flipped through the pages twice, looking for the fish poem, but there were no verses of any kind. For the most part, it seemed to be filled with complaints and cynical commentary about the server hierarchy. How unlike a server to be so petty, thought Elenn. Then she noticed on one of the pages a name written in familiar characters. It was "Tilke," or at least some name that used the same characters. She tried to recall the possibilities from her writing lessons. Alternative readings might have been *Tilka*, or *Pilke*, or *Pilka*. At any rate it was definitely the same characters used in Tilke's name. She sat to read what it said.

> *I am sick today with memories of you, my friend.*
> *What I had managed to avoid thinking about for*

many moon cycles came back to me when I heard some newly ordained young servers talking piously about their devotion to the Beh. It was as if they were reciting your own words. What a grievous error you have made, my Pilka. Didn't you know that this server path is just a diversion, something to keep us from going mad while we wait for the sweeter madness of ro-raving? How could the Beh be interested in anything a server has to give? She sleeps for us, we live for Her, it is enough. What drove you to attempt to gain further favor? Whatever it was, Pilka, it has brought nothing but misery. For you, the loss of passing. But I see your flaw recurring around me constantly. These young servers come in, eager to shed their nameliness, but anyone can see how quickly they are competing to show off their devotion. It's sickening. It's their mentors' fault. La'ult and the other ro-servers don't even know enough to correct them. Half the servers here don't even see things deteriorating. Mekkun still hasn't compensated me for the tools I got her. She'd better pay me back soon or I'll remind her when it's most embarrassing.

The journal went on from there, focusing on gossip and accusations with no mention of Tilke, or Pilke or whoever it was. Elenn didn't know what was more shocking, the un-serverlike attitude of the journal, or the mention of this other Tilke individual losing her passing-of-life.

Elenn was so tired of thinking about her future. She had wanted nothing more than to resolve her insecurities and submit her name to the Beyan temple. But the more she contemplated and explored the steps to joining the servers, the more she became discouraged instead of inspired. Now she was getting this unpleasant picture of server life that was just as gossipy and contemptible as any experience among the masters. The only thing that enabled her to persevere was her love of the exercises. She knew that the exercises were pleasing to Lern Beyana. Only by becoming a server would she have the chance to make the exercises her life's focus. Maybe it had been a mistake to come looking for help in the writings of old servers. Maybe her time would be better spent doing the exercises that inspired her to consider server life in the first place.

Elenn situated herself on the floor to do a mind-stilling exercise right there in the library. She had not seen a single uedin pass the doorway to the room where the server collection was held. She would be undisturbed there.

The room was absolutely quiet. She could hear her own pulse. She concentrated on her breathing. It felt good to be still. Normally Elenn could engage in mind-stilling exercise for a good part of the night without falling asleep, but she had been thinking too much about her decision and had not slept well for days. In the quietness and the isolation there in the corner room of the library, she began to feel a sinking sensation. One was not supposed to fall asleep during a mind-stilling exercise, but she was too tired. Her head leaned comfortably back against the soft grainy texture of the saltstone.

In the dream, Elenn and Tilke were in the Quarterhouse main building, but it was now a papermaking operation. And they weren't Elenn and Tilke —they were unnamed again, dressed in the simple garments of the unnamed. Nobody else was there, and there was no one to show them how, but they seemed to know the process for lifting the pressed, wet paper from the screens and laying it in sheets on the drying beds. Tilke—who wasn't "Tilke" yet—spoke to her, saying, "So the unnamed likes the exercises?" It sounded like teasing, and it made Elenn—who wasn't "Elenn" yet—feel angry. Then not-yet-Elenn spoke spitefully to her companion, saying, "You're going to get the name of an old prophet who never made it to Ceulan." Then not-yet-Tilke said, "There's no such thing as a prophet—prophets are only characters in the old myths." And then not-yet-Elenn said, "How do we know what to call myths? How do we know even Lern Beyana is not a myth?" As she said this, not-yet-Elenn looked down and saw that the wet paper she was picking up from the screens already had writing on it. It was in an old calligraphy style, and she quickly recognized it as the verses of Yemel. Then she heard not-yet-Tilke saying in a mournful voice, "Lern Beyana is not a myth." And not-yet-Elenn said, "How do you know this, Pilka?" She called her Pilka, but she did not know why. And when she looked up, her companion's eyes were wide and round, and tears began to fall from them in streams, and her companion said, "Because Lern Beyana speaks to me directly." Then not-yet-Elenn said "Lern Beyana does not speak." Then she looked down and saw that her hands were covered with the purplish blood of a dog, and her mouth was full of blood. And she knelt in front of her companion and brought her hands to her face in shame. Then not-yet-Tilke reached out and touched the head of not-yet-Elenn, and her skullwomb came off of her head painlessly as if it were a hat. She felt it come off her head, and she looked up in wonder, but instead of seeing her skullwomb in her friend's hand, there was one of the simple wooden bowls from Quarterhouse. It was empty, except for the teardrops falling from the face of not-yet-Tilke. And she knew that Tilke was telling the truth, that she was spoken to directly from the Lern. Then she asked, "Are those the tears of Lern Beyana?" And not-yet-Tilke replied, "No. They are your *tears."*

Elenn's eyes opened as a shocking realization took hold of her. She was immediately awake, her heart pounding and her mind in panic. She leaned forward and looked around at the shelves. In the space of an instant, a terrible thing had conveyed itself to her. A truth had settled upon her. Even as she mentally grappled to reclaim her wakeful bearings, she felt it, unthinkable, yet penetrating her bones. A single word, but in it a complete damnation: barren. Without knowing why she knew, she knew. It was as if the message had been delivered to her from the future.

She pushed herself against the wall and stood up. She looked down at her feet. It was unreal, unbelievable to her. She skewered her brow and looked around. What was happening? She knew that the dream she had been having was over, and she was awake now. But somehow she felt she had woken up to a different reality where things were plummeting into a terrifying state of wrongness. She looked at her hands. She saw the hands of a barren. She didn't want to own them. She didn't want to be in this body. An involuntary shaking started to come over her. She felt the muscles in her face curl up around her eyes. She felt a convulsion and heard the sound of a strange wail come up from her chest as a wave of grief erupting from inside of her. She was too confused to cry, and yet now tears began to pour in streams from her eyes. She couldn't even see the room around her. It made no sense to her.

Barren. No life in her skullwomb. What did it mean to have no life to carry and release? What was the source of this horror being visited upon her? She had never considered what barren really meant. It was not just the absence of something. The absence of something, a simple loss, tallies toward the neutral zero. This was rather a horrendous, unacceptable thing.

Her life force would not go to an embryo in her skullwomb. No wetuedin would come from her. Where would her life force go? She heard a horrible groan come from her own mouth, but it seemed like someone else's voice—not her. She collapsed on the floor. She felt the cold stone and the gritty dirt under her cheek. It felt strange. It felt like someone else's flesh and someone else's cheekbone mashing against the stone surface.

"*THIS IS NOT ME!*" she heard herself scream. The loudness of it startled her. She had to be quiet. She couldn't fall apart like this. They would hear her and come running. *Be quiet! Don't cry! Don't make noise!*

What if they already heard her? The temple collection room was pretty far away from the main hall, but they might have heard her scream. What would she say if they came running? She had to be quiet. She coughed and cleared her throat. She stood up and wiped her face with her hands. For a moment, she felt a quiet emptiness inside. The saltstone walls around her glistened. She felt a strange numbness. The white sand-crystaled stone looked lovely and soft.

Elenn tried to recover herself, recalling all her training and discipline. She stood and slowly wiped the dirt and wetness from her face. She forced herself to take some deep breaths. She used her attention to relax her lungs, which kept trying to contract and heave into sobs again. Her head felt feverish, but instead of putting her hand to her forehead, she directed it coldly to the thin volume on the table, lifted the booklet and returned it to the shelf. Her eyes lingered on shelves, poured over the shadows, noticed the dust on the floor. No matter where she looked, no matter what she thought about, the word 'barren' was ringing in her head. Do not break down again! Do not! Breathe! Stand up!

She was glad to see that the corridors were still empty. As she entered the main hallway of the library, a few trapped birds flew back and forth over her head. Did they ever find their way out? The thought of being trapped suddenly stung her, forcing her attention back to the thought she was trying to suppress. *What will I do? What will I do?*

When she turned the corner into the lobby, she unexpectedly came face to face with a uniformed guard. There was light enough to see the guard's face, and she looked familiar. It was Master Deben.

"Oh, excuse me, ..." Deben didn't recognize Elenn at first. But she saw the unmistakable look of grief on Elenn's face.

"Are you all right young uedin?" she asked. Then she recognized her. "Aren't you the newly-named I met at the lichen fields? What was your name again?"

Seeing kind regard in Deben's face was too much for her. She could not hold back. She gasped in an awkward, pathetic attempt to retain her composure. Master Deben reached out with sincere concern.

"Are you all right, young uedin? What's the name?"

Elenn collapsed into a heap at the feet of the astonished guard, and like a dam breaking, violent sobbing overtook her. She could not bear to speak her own detestable name.

Domas at the Infirmary

The infirmary had the most brightly lit interior of any building in the capital. Domas had only been inside a few times, but on every occasion she was impressed by the carefully planned use of lamps, ceiling windows and mirror panels. An apprentice medic led her to the laboratory where an older medic was sterilizing some small tools made of metal wire and glass filigree.

"Excuse me, Master Ferin," said the apprentice to the older medic, "Master Domas is asking if she may speak with you and observe the barren patient."

"Oh, yes, of course." Ferin looked up. "Master Domas, I received your message. As you know, the barren individual has been here for nearly twenty days now. She is going to live, but her condition is dismal. We finished our blood and tissue tests yesterday. I had an extra copy of the report written out for you and the council. I'd be happy to explain any of it to you. Why don't we go take a look for now?"

"Thank you, Master Ferin." said Domas. They walked to the back of the lab and entered a small room with normal, dim lighting. The barren uedin was lying on a cot, semi-conscious. Her breath was shallow and uneasy. Domas could not help feeling overwhelming pity at the sight of the tormented and ailing figure.

"As you can see right away, her enlarged body frame indicates advanced stages of barren syndrome. We haven't seen this level of affliction in a barren uedin any time during my career. Usually they die before reaching this state… Or, if not, they're long gone into the wilderness."

"Did the tests tell you anything new?" asked Domas.

"We've known that part of the barren derangement is caused by abnormal levels of skullsap—no surprise really, it's the same thing that happens to healthy uedin when we come into ecstasy. In healthy uedin, the developed embryo metabolizes the parent's skull sap and only when it begins to manufacture some of its own skullsap, when it is soon to be born, does the parent uedin experience the effect of excess. That's what functions as a trigger for ecstacy and pilgrimage. Without any embryo at all, the skullsap of the adult uedin is constantly redistributed into the circulatory system and leads to barren syndrome. With this patient, we tried to reduce skullsap content in the blood by draining it directly from the umbilical vesicle."

"You mean the skullsap vein?"

"Yes. We tried to stop reabsorption of skullsap into the body, but the patient went into withdrawal."

"Withdrawal? But the barren don't need their skullsap, do they?"

"They don't need it for an embryo, but after their body becomes accustomed to it, they become physiologically dependent on very high levels. It's all in recent notes about the syndrome."

"Very interesting. Is the patient in any better condition now than when she was brought here?" asked Domas.

"There's nothing we can do about the derangement. This one has permanent damage. We have her on some sedatives to make her more manageable, but that's only intended as a temporary measure. We really don't want to start a precedent by keeping a barren in custody through the use of sedatives."

"Thank you very much, Master Ferin," said Domas. "I suspect that the council will only ask you to keep her sedated until she can be escorted from the capital and released. I intend to recommend as much." Domas had one more question. "Master Ferin, may I ask your opinion on something?"

"Certainly, Master."

"I understand what causes barren derangement, but I don't understand why we see the barren becoming a danger. Ro-ecstasy is not entirely different from the derangement of barren syndrome… yet we would never see a ro-uedin in ecstasy threatening harm to anyone. Have you thought about that?"

"I have my theory," said Ferin. "I believe the barren can't produce enough skullsap to satisfy their own craving. The craving, together with the derangement, results in a dangerous combination. That's why we hear of the horrible incidents associated with them."

"I don't suppose you've included that in your writings on the subject, Master Ferin?"

"No. It's only conjecture. But if you think the council would find it useful, please feel free to pass it on."

"Very well. Your work is much appreciated, Master Ferin. I will let you know what the council decides."

Domas took a final, silent look at the barren individual lying in front of her. What disturbed her the most was the tortured condition of the poor uedin's feet. They were raw and infected from more than a moon cycle of unprotected wandering outside the capital. What an unimaginable, awful life—the horror of not having life in one's skullcap, followed by the misery and physical suffering of deterioration and wandering in the wilderness. While she respected Master Ferin for her work, Domas would never be able to regard life with such detachment. What uedin wants to think that her passing-of-life is determined by some change of her brain fluids? How could one work within a model that separated itself from the connection with Lern Beyana and Her dependence on the uedin and their ongoing procreation? She would have never made a good medic.

Domas was quietly reviewing Master Ferin's report that evening before heading off to the council meeting when she received an unexpected visit.

"Please pardon my intrusion," said the voice from behind the door tarp. She looked up from the papers with mild aggravation. It was a young voice, one of her advisees she was certain.

"Yes, please enter," she called back and turned to see who was there. It was indeed one of her advisees, the newly-named

Elenn. Elenn was a very bright young uedin, but she had a strong introspective habit and seemed obsessively interested in exercises and fanciful ideas about server culture.

"I'm sorry to interrupt your studies, Master Domas," said Elenn.

"Please feel welcome, young uedin. I'm not really involved in any studies here—I just have to review something for a meeting I'll be attending shortly. I'm afraid I don't have much time. How can I help you?"

"It's about my choice of assignment, Master." When Domas had spoken to her before, she had the distinct impression that Elenn was considering joining the server community. There was nothing wrong with that, of course, but masters were not in any kind of place to advise favorably or unfavorably about the option of becoming a server. Domas had been in that awkward predicament a few times before. The servers themselves, of course, offered little support or encouragement to newly-named who considered entering their ranks.

"Young Elenn, I'm afraid this is not the best time to discuss such an important decision. I will be leaving for a council meeting soon."

"Master Domas, I won't require any of your time. I've made my decision."

"Oh?"

"Yes, Master. I've decided to join the guards."

Domas looked at her in disbelief. It was a most unimaginable choice for such a solemn and introspective individual.

"The guards? Young Master Elenn, what ever put the idea of joining the guards into your mind?"

"Do you think I'm unsuitable for the guards, Master Domas?" asked Elenn. The look in her eyes revealed just the slightest hint of hurt feelings.

"No, Elenn," Domas adjusted her reaction to show respect for the newly-named's choice. "If you feel certain that you want to be a guard master, I'm sure you'll be quite competent. It's just not what I expected to hear from you. Are you already in contact with one of the guard stations?"

"Yes, Master, with the station right here in the Flatpools District."

"Really? Well, that should be an easy transition for you. Perhaps we'll see you from time to time"

Elenn did not comment.

"So then you must have determined that server life was not for you," said Domas.

"Server life?" Elenn was looking back at her blankly.

"Come now," said Domas, "We both know that you were thinking of going into the temple community."

"It's not for me," said Elenn. "I heard that once you enter the temple you never get to come out, and every day is the same."

Domas smiled. The masters were probably a little guilty of instilling their own biases in the unnamed. This one hadn't seemed to be the type who would be so easily influenced. "Well perhaps I was misreading you before. I thought you were very serious about becoming a server."

"I was a little confused about where I might fit, but now that I've settled on the guard masters, I'm sure I've made the right decision," said Elenn without emotion. Domas could sense the resolve in Elenn's voice, but it seemed to be coming from a place of resignation. There was something heartbreaking about it. Yet there was no way that she, a master, could recommend that Elenn explore the server path. Maybe the life of the guards would suit her. It did involve discipline, uniformity of character, and mental focus—all of which were, to some degree, server characteristics. It was probably one of the less busy-minded of the paths of masterhood.

"You've been a very kind and generous advisor, Master Domas, so I wanted you to be the first to know. But I don't need to use any more of your time. I'll take my leave now."

Domas stood up to bid her proper farewell. "Congratulations, Elenn," she said, "You'll soon be on your way to a fine career."

"Thank you, Master," Elenn answered, and left quickly.

Domas' eyes lingered on the door momentarily as she absorbed the idea of Elenn becoming a capital guard. Life seemed so much more complicated and unpredictable for these new generations. She sometimes forgot how old she was, but then there were times like this when she realized that she was ready to let the younger masters take over. A day was coming when she was going to be able to put it all away and prepare for her pilgrimage. Ah, but till then, she was on the council, there were hard issues to resolve, and her duties were going to require every bit of serious thinking she had to offer. With that in mind, she picked up Ferin's report and left for the council meeting.

Tilke and Elenn Choose Assignments

Fog lay around the sunken field behind Quarterhouse. Tilke walked down the path along the greenbark trees to the pavilion where she and Elenn had arranged to meet. She hadn't seen Elenn for days, and when she had seen her, they hadn't had a chance to talk. She was thrilled when she found the note in her message box suggesting the meeting. Elenn didn't know that Tilke had decided to submit her name to the temple servers. She hadn't told anybody yet, not even her advisor, Master Leksa. A shorter moon cycle from now she and Elenn would be together in training.

How would she explain it? Something amazing had happened. She had gone back a second time to visit the paper mill. Master Karam hadn't been there that day, but the other masters had told Tilke to observe and explore as much as she liked. She spent a lot of time just looking at the display samples. The papers were beautiful. There were so many different shades—lovely green and golden-hued papers. Tilke guessed at what the paper masters used for making the dyes. Some of the samples featured flecks of crumbled flower petals or other interesting stringy bits added to the mash.

There was one particular large sheet of plain, undyed paper that the masters had on display as if it were something very special. She had hardly taken notice of it at first, but then it caught her eye again. How odd, Tilke thought, to mount and display the most ordinary product so prominently when the mill produced so many exceptional and gorgeous papers. There was a stack of heavy paper dyed to vivid purple shades. She gently lifted the sheets, admiring the variations of rich color. When she looked up, her eye landed again on the plain white sample. This time she took a minute to stare at it. What was it about that white sheet that drew her attention? It was something both annoying and appealing. It stood out in whiteness, demanding attention, and yet upon recognition of its ordinariness was immediately disappointing. There was a small stool near the table. Tilke put it in front of the sample and sat to look at it. She gazed at the plain surface. The irritation she felt was something inside herself. What was it? Plainness. The white paper was absolutely plain. It stirred an unpleasant feeling, a natural dislike for that which is dull. But the dullness she was reacting to, Tilke sensed, was a judgment of her own mind. Staring at the sheet at length, Tilke began to realize that the irritant was her own demanding nature, and that the paper itself reflected nothing but the beautiful quality of its pure whiteness. Its clean vacancy seemed to hold some secret promise of relief. Whatever it was that she liked about the paper mill and the work of the masters there, it was evident in that big sheet of plain paper. It was pure, and basic, and down to its element.

As Tilke stared and stared into the white plain she became strangely focused. The paper looked very new; it must have been only recently pressed. From that conscious thought, her mind slipped into a tranquil blankness. Looking into the field of white, she momentarily forgot what she was looking at. She was close enough that most of her vision was contained by the surface before her. Its edges might as well have stretched indefinitely in all directions, for she felt there was nothing to see but the ever-extending whiteness, as though she were looking at infinity. Then, as if she had either discovered or been fooled into some trick of relativity, she found herself wondering—was light reflecting *off* of the white surface, or was it emanating *from* it? From a world of shapes and complexity, was she drawn *into* the eternal—or was it the eternal from which she looked *backwards* into shapes and complexity? Both worlds felt softer and lighter at their meeting point. Gradually she withdrew from the trance and remembered where she was. She rose from the stool with her mind in a daze. She turned around and looked at the empty room. A quality of softness filled everything she looked at. She quietly walked toward the door to leave. As she stepped across the soft floor and lifted the soft door tarp, she heard in her head the sound of her own voice reciting the names of Lern Beyana. Instead of an outgoing communication to the Lern, the syllables seemed to form a stream on which thoughts flowed backward into her, communicating a subtle message of delicate satisfaction. She hadn't recited the Names since the time she had been on her way to the lichen fields with Elenn. She began to whisper the names so that she would in fact be reciting them, not just going over them in her head. As she listened to her own whispering voice, she had a mysterious feeling as though she were reciting the names together with hundreds and hundreds of other uedin. She was one among untold multitudes—more than the population of many generations—reciting the names at the same time. She knew that those multitudes were the servers.

Since that afternoon Tilke had thought repeatedly about how Elenn had told her in the lichen field that she *was* a server—not that she should be or could be a server—but that she *was* a server.

Now she knew that Elenn was right. Tilke knew she was a server. There was no decision to make.

The figure of Elenn became visible through the fog. She was coming down the ramp looking out into the fog that covered the open Quarterhouse field. How slender and stately she looked, thought Tilke. She already had the appearance and bearing of a server. As Elenn approached, Tilke saw that she wore an expression of seriousness. She was glad that instead of rushing from the paper mill to tell Elenn about her revelation, she had reserved it for this special moment.

Their eyes met with a balanced understanding of mutual respect and affection. They both knew that this meeting was too important for their normal casual behavior, and they raised hands to face in an exchange of formal greeting. Tilke looked into her friend's eyes and saw wisdom and compassion. Maybe Elenn thought she was still opting for the paper mill—her look of resignation suggested that she had made peace with disappointment. Tilke decided to speak first.

"Elenn, it's very good to see you. It feels like such a long time since we've talked. It was hard not to come looking for you."

"It does seem like it's been a long time." said Elenn. "I guess we've both had a lot to think about."

Tilke's face radiated with happiness. "Elenn," she said, "I've decided to go with you!"

The look in Elenn's eye changed, as if she were looking inside herself. But she remained very calm. Tilke marveled at her centeredness—she must have spent their time apart in very focused exercises.

Tilke continued, "I was at the paper mill two days ago when I had a realization—a vision really. And now I know that you were right—that I belong with the servers." Tilke looked for some sign of gladness in Elenn's face, but there didn't seem to be any. Was Elenn concerned that she had talked her into something that she didn't really want?

"What's wrong?" she asked. "This is my own decision, Elenn. Don't be afraid that you've influenced me here. I feel very sure about this. Aren't you glad that we're going to be together?" Her excitement began to collapse as she perceived the delay in Elenn's response.

"We aren't going to be together, Tilke," said Elenn in a small whisper. She sounded very sad.

Tilke looked back at her friend for a moment, confused by what she was hearing. "What? We're not going to be together?"

She didn't understand. "Elenn—I am going to join the Beyan temple! I submitted my name last night!"

Elenn turned her head to peer into the fog over the field. "And I submitted my name yesterday also—to the capital guards."

Tilke stared at her friend in disbelief. What was this?

"That's crazy, Elenn!" she cried in anger, "What are you saying!"

"I'm not joining the servers!" Elenn yelled back and glared into Tilke's eyes. "I'm going to join the guards at the Flatpools District station! I've already made my choice—there's nothing you can do about it!"

Had Elenn rejected the server path because of that foolish fear she had about her own nameliness? "Elenn..." Tilke pleaded. She didn't know how to express her hurt and confusion. "How could you?"

Elenn looked about in different directions, trying to appear distracted and impatient. She said nothing.

Tilke felt sick with the betrayal. "You're going to join the guards—after all this?" Tilke was filled with disgust and disappointment.

"I can't explain my choice, Tilke. I'm sorry."

"You can't explain! Do you think your ideas are too hard for me to grasp? They're not! I understood all along—you never hid it—you were afraid you were too *'namely.'* But I'll tell you what I think— your ideas are stupid and wrong."

"Tilke, I'm sorry... I just can't."

Tilke looked at her. Was she really sorry? She did look miserable. How could she have done this? Humility was one thing. It would not be good to join the servers with a prideful attitude. But to relinquish the whole idea out of concern about nameliness? Did Elenn think there was something noble in that?

"You didn't even want to take a name because it was too conceited. And now you've rejected Lern Beyana because you think it would be too *namely* to become a server. Your ideas are twisted. Your constant worrying about being namely has become a conceit. You're the most namely one of all." Tilke felt sick. She turned to walk away.

"Tilke!" Elenn protested. Tilke stopped momentarily to allow her whatever final lame apology she wanted to make. "Tilke... you'll be a great server! Tilke, I'm so proud of you!" The words rang empty in Tilke's ears. She walked briskly from the pavilion and back up the hill without looking back.

Part 3

APPRENTICESHIP

Masters Gossip over Lunch

It had been seventeen combined moon cycles since Namesgiving, and the novade was nearing its end. Signs of the coming nine-year monsoon were in the air. They included a certain stillness, the dry heat, and, because of the traditions of the capital, a general silence. The Quarterhouse masters largely let go of protocol during the last year of a novade. Nearly all the newly-named were gone away to various assignments. The halls and dormitories were empty and unpleasantly quiet. It was always a particularly strange time for Quarterhouse masters since there wasn't much to do but maintain the facilities and wait for rain.

Master Benar sat at a table in the dining hall with a heaping plate of roasted squash. How nice it was, she thought, to be able to dispense with the usual table manners. She happily sprinkled salt and bitterspice onto her mountain of squash while absently humming to herself. Then it came to her that it might be very pleasant to compose a little poem. She dug in her pocket for a scrap of paper and a coalstick. She wrote with slow deliberation, taking breaks to gulp her food.

> *The newly-named are gone away*
> *The masters sleep a little later*
> *The dinner plate holds a little more*

Yes, that seemed like a very nice start. She needed one more "little" of something to complete the form. What could it be? she thought. *'The empty quarterhouse seems a little bigger'* or *'we can't help wishing it were a little noisier'*?

"Master Benar, may we join you?" It was Leksa and Domas—teaching masters. Benar stuffed the paper and coalstick back into her pocket.

"Oh yes, please, Master Leksa and Master Domas, please do." They sat down at the table.

"How are you faring with this heat, Master Benar?" asked Domas.

"I'm not a young uedin anymore. I should know what to expect by now, but I must admit I'm always unprepared for the heat," said Benar with a laugh. "I do, however, enjoy the leisure."

"Master Benar," said Leksa, "I heard that three of the newly-named are going to stay and apprentice as caretakers."

"It's true," said Benar. "Now let me see, what were the young uedins' names? Kebel and, um, what were the others?"

"So you're not working very closely with them I take it?"

"The younger masters were eager to work with them, so I'm letting them take over, for the most part."

"Pano was deciding between staying on as a caretaker or joining the workermasters of the western outfields," commented Leksa.

"Perhaps she opted for the farming masters then," said Benar. "Pano is not one of our three new caretakers."

"Was Pano one of your advisees, Master Leksa?" asked Domas.

"Yes indeed. I only had two advisees. Pano and Tilke."

"Tilke was one of yours?" asked Domas with some interest.

"Yes. She was going to apprentice at the paper mill. But then one morning I had a message that she was joining the central temple servers. It was a bit of a surprise."

"Well, that's very interesting." said Domas.

"Did you have some interaction with Tilke?" asked Leksa.

"No, I never talked with her. But some of us were curious about her taking of name."

Benar swallowed a mouthful and said, "That's right, Master Domas, I remember you and Master Lemeh talking about that." She had a bit of roasted squash on her upper lip. "You thought her name was a recurrence of an earlier server name, right?"

"Yes—'Pilka.' Did that ever occur to you, Master Leksa?" asked Domas.

Leksa stopped and regarded the idea. "No …" she said thoughtfully. "No, Master Benar, I never considered that. *Tilke*—hmm, yes, come to think of it, that would have been a recurrence of 'Pilka.' Pilka was a server as well, wasn't she? Well, history is your specialty, Master Domas."

"Is there something significant about the name Pilka?" Benar asked.

"Pilka was a high-ranking server before the Claybridge Period." explained Domas. "She was at the center of great unrest and scandal in the central temple. In the end they expelled her for her fanaticism."

"Well, my Tilke won't be any trouble. I found her to be a very sensible young uedin." said Leksa. "I was hoping she might stay at Quarterhouse, but she wasn't interested in a tutor or caretaker assignment. We got her set up to visit the paper mill. I thought that might seem a little boring for Tilke—a very bright newly-named—but it actually looked like it was going to go that way. And then, all the sudden, she up and decided to become a server. What a coincidence if she had a recurrance of a server name, and she went to become a server. I admit I'm glad she didn't ask me anything about it."

"It *is* awkward when an advisee wants to be a server, though, isn't it? You're lucky your Tilke just sent you the message without asking you to counsel her," said Domas. "I had one this time who seemed quite intent on serverhood. Every time I saw her coming I felt completely unprepared to deal with her. Then in the end she changed her mind and joined the guards!" The masters chuckled at this unlikely switch.

"Isn't that just how they are, the newly-named?" said Benar with a laugh.

"The guards have a tougher job these days," said Leksa.

"Yes they do. They don't have much background for dealing with this problem with the barren," said Domas. Benar was surprised to hear Domas mention the topic there in the dining hall. Since the Namesgiving, the masters mentioned it so casually—as if it were as common as a foot rash.

"Master Domas, I trust you know what happened to the individual in Master Ferin's report that you shared at the council meeting?"

"Yes I heard about her. Very sad news, wasn't it."

"Was it a barren uedin?" asked Benar cautiously. She wasn't sure how much she really wanted to hear about it.

"Yes, a very severe case," said Domas. "I observed her in the infirmary a few short moon cycles ago. She was so pathetic—it was quite disturbing."

"What happened to her?" asked Benar.

"The guards found her body at the Haka Cliffs about six days ago," said Leksa. "The medics confirmed it was the same one Master Ferin had studied for her report. She apparently had either fallen or jumped to her death."

Master Domas said nothing. Benar finished her meal and stood up. "Well, if you will please excuse me," she said. "A few of the younger masters are showing the apprentices how to put up shutters on the dormitory windows for the coming rain. I think I may go check on them."

"It was very nice to see you again, Master Benar." said Leksa. Domas nodded politely.

Benar touched the paper in her pocket as she walked away. She had decided on a different line to conclude her poem. It would be 'A *caretaker's cares are a little heavier.*' It didn't really fit with the beginning, but nobody would ever look at it anyhow.

The Arrival of Rains

The capital baked under the sun, waiting for the Great Rains of the novade's end. For days there had been only occasional dust-laden wind, hot and offering no relief. All activity had come to a halt. There was nothing to do but wait for the Rains.

Elenn walked on the dirt alley that ran behind the guard station in the Flatpools District. A lizard, lethargic in the sun, didn't even scurry away when she stepped over it. Elenn had no particular destination. She was in the fourth longer moon cycle of training. All the new conscripts knew to report to the station at the first sign of clouds. They had completed the new retaining wall on the inside drystream that led to Quarterhouse. Most of the guards were in the station residence, trying to get extra sleep since they knew they would have to work day and night once the Rains came. The streets were empty and the capital in general felt desolate.

In some ways, Elenn's assignment with the guards was working out better than she had anticipated. Master Deben was able to work closely with her, just as she had promised. Her interest in shifting exercises from before taking name was very helpful in training, and her academic strength, rare among the guard masters, impressed her superiors. But when training sessions and duty periods were over, Elenn made little effort to join the camaraderie of the young guards. There were six newly-named in training, including herself. Guards were not celebrated in uedin history or granted much prestige in the capital, but they had a quiet sense of purpose and pride that they kept to themselves. If Elenn had not once dreamed of joining the servers, she might have been quite satisfied to embrace the quietly dignified work of the guards. But when they sang guard songs, she thought of Tilke chanting the names of Lern Beyana; when they practiced maneuvers, she thought of Tilke achieving new levels of skill in the shifting exercises.

When Deben had taken Elenn from the library to the station to give her water and make sure she was all right, she had pressed Elenn to reveal the problem that had overwhelmed her. Deben had a gift for dealing with the distraught. Elenn remembered the time she and Tilke watched Deben talking gently with the barren up in the lichen field.

Deben told Elenn that her dream was a result of natural anxieties and stresses. The taking of name was an overwhelming event for those who appreciated the responsibilities of selfhood. Deben believed that many of the masters around the capital spoke too casually about the barren syndrome, and that it planted fear in the minds of the child-uedin. She thought there were probably many newly-named who were wrongly convinced that they were barren. She thought that what they had seen in the lichen fields had been very traumatic, and that Elenn's dream was just a nightmare.

Elenn took consolation where she could. She didn't believe in Deben's reassurances, but she appreciated her compassion and good intentions. Not wanting to be deprived of those, she would pretend to believe.

She longed to recite the Names of the Lern, which gave her comfort. She had known from her earliest days at Quarterhouse that Lern Beyana was fragile and delicate. All devotion and manner of exercise had to proceed from a peaceful mind. Invoking Her with thoughts of fear or need was sacrilege and could erode the relationship between uedin and Lern. Knowing this, Elenn tried to put her torment away so that she might be able to do what she loved the most, but indeed she carried too much distress in her mind.

She looked up at the dark, hazy atmosphere. Instead of the Names, she repeated a poem about the passing-of-life that she remembered learning from the Quarterhouse masters.

> *My heart is too tired to beat*
> *And yet with what strength does it ache.*
> *When will I go? No matter,*
> *It is not soon enough!*

She didn't remember the name of the poet, just that it was a Quarterhouse master long ago. Recalling the poem only made her feel sorry for herself, but it was stuck in her head. She paused on the street momentarily to feel the hot, dirt-laden wind flick against her face and arms.

Later that afternoon Elenn was sitting alone in front of the supply house, sharpening tools to kill time. She heard someone beating on the wooden clapper board at the station. She stood and looked around. There were black clouds on the northern horizon.

When Elenn got to the station, Master Henik, a third-generation guard, was already handing out rain gear and shovels. Henik sent all the other guards off in different directions except for one other regular guard and the trainees.

"I'll take those two with me. Master Ribol, take the others through eastgate and keep watch on the levee while the marsh fills up." She turned to Elenn and the other trainee standing beside her. "You two can come with me. We'll be watching the new retaining wall for the stream that runs along the north."

They grabbed the rain gear and shovels and rushed after Henik, pulling wax-cloth capes over them as they ran.

"Master Elenn—glad to be working with you," said the other trainee.

"You're Master Simol, right?" shouted Elenn.

"Right."

"Seems funny to put on these rain capes when it's still hot and dry, doesn't it?"

"They say once the rain breaks, it falls in torrents."

They jogged after Henik as she went along the inside of the capital wall until they reached the north gate. They went out and along the outside of the capital wall toward the northeast corner, closest to Flatpools. Now when they looked behind them they could see billowing black clouds getting larger in the sky above the hill country.

One large drystream ran directly to the capital from the northwest. It ran along the north wall and then divided into smaller streams, some of which flowed directly through openings in the wall and led to the various hatching pools of the capital. Other branches emptied into an area northeast of the capital which became a marshland with every Great Rains. Of the streams that flowed through the capital itself, the largest fed the Quarterhouse hatching pool, a large and shallow pond always referred to as "the flatpool." Other streams ran to other areas of the capital and were dammed at various hatching pools around which the other domiciles were built up. All streams made their way to the canyon east of the capital where one large drystream reformed and led around and southward. The Clay Bridge crossed it just below the capital's south gate. The Great Rains always brought some standard flooding damage. A more serious concern was that the streams would overflow and change their direction. It often happened, and if the flow couldn't be diverted back to the hatching pools by the time the Lake Ceulan floodwater reached the capital, wetuedin could be lost. Once the Rains began, the guards would be working day and night to prevent such a disaster.

Henik led Elenn and Simol along the bank of the deep drystream. They came to the spot where a retaining wall had been built to keep the stream in place once it filled up. Great Rains in recent novades had shown the river wanting to wash right up against the capital wall at that spot. The bottom of the stream bed was still dry, with dead weeds lying in patches, but they all knew a downpour was imminent from the eerie brown color that the sky was taking on above their heads.

They could see some Northgate District guards further up on the same side of the drystream checking on a section of the inside bank that had been reinforced with stacked rock in some previous novade.

"Sometimes if the Rains blow in from the northwest they hit the hill country before the capital. Water will rush in the streams before any actual rainfall," said Henik. "When that happens, the Ceulan floodwaters come early—sometimes on the second day of the Rains."

This time, however, the storm appeared to be arriving from due north. A flash of lightning turned everything white for an instant and a heavy explosion of thunder crashed above them. Simol and Elenn both jumped when the thunder cracked. Storms were known to come annually in wet seasons for the early years of every novade, but their generation had not experienced them since they were too young to remember.

They could see the comb of rainfall rushing toward them. Small puffs of dust and steam bounced up as the first bullets of rain struck the hot surface of the ground. Then in an instant they were completely engulfed by heavy downpour.

The rain was like nothing Elenn could have imagined. It fell in great sheets. In seconds the view of the exterior capital wall was obliterated as a plane of gray vertical lines replaced their field of vision. Against the drumming of the rain on the hood of her cape, Elenn heard Master Henik shouting. She looked at her. Henik was smiling and yelling through the rain, but Elenn couldn't hear a word.

"*What?*" she yelled. She watched Henik's mouth move again, but she only guessed what she was saying when Henik pointed to the bottom of the drystream. Already, inches of brown water were rushing over the rocks. Simol's face beamed with excitement.

In the hours that followed, what had been a deep dry gully turned into a river of muddy water. The retaining wall that the guards had worked on during the past moon cycle appeared to be solidly resisting the force of the current. They stood in the rain, watching it. The rushing river of brown, muddy water was almost hypnotizing.

Suddenly a figure in rain gear came running from downstream. At first, Elenn couldn't see who it was. Then she caught sight of the guard's face under the hood of her wax-cloth cape. It was Master Deben. She shouted something in Henik's ear. Henik looked toward the spot upstream on the inside where the Northgate guards had been keeping watch. Deben must have checked in with them while making her rounds. Henik waved Elenn and Simol over to her and then yelled to their faces through the rain.

"*Master Deben was just with the Northgate guards! They need help over there! The old retaining wall's getting washed away!*" The trainees nodded and followed her. They ran along the capital wall to get to the trouble spot. Elenn ran with them, taking care to keep her footing on the muddy ground. She had never before walked on such an unsolid surface.

As they moved eastward on the strip of solid land between the capital wall and the stream, the streambed itself seemed to be wider and shallower as it neared the marsh. But the rush of brown water in the stream was near the breaching point. Once that powerful current started tearing away the old retaining wall, Elenn could not imagine how the guards could possibly stop it.

They reached the place where a constant current of water was pounding away at the retaining wall. The guards there had already settled on a strategy and were hard at work. They were breaking stone blocks from the capital wall and carrying them to the spot where the section of retaining wall was getting washed out. There they were carefully tossing them down into the muddy current to form a crude deterrent to stop the erosion. Elenn couldn't believe they were dismantling a portion of the capital wall to get the blocks, but it made sense. After the Great Rains, they could retrieve them and repair the wall.

They worked for hours breaking off the stone blocks and carrying them to the bank to toss or roll them down, hoping that they were positioning them effectively to retard the cutting force of the current. One could only carry the heavy blocks for a short while, so the guards rotated tasks.

Though it was a critical race against the current, the work itself was monotonous. Physically nearing exhaustion, Elenn felt her pulse pounding in her chest and head as she broke mortar and pulled blocks from a row on the capital wall. The poem she had been thinking of earlier came back to her. Feeling her own pounding heart, she thought of the poet who said her heart was tired of beating. *My heart is too tired to beat, And yet with what strength does it ache. When will I go? No matter, It is not soon enough!*

Within days, she knew, wetuedin would be swimming down to the flatpools. Over the last novade, they had been born of ro-uedin gone to Lake Ceulan for their passing. The masters speculated that wetuedin development reached a point of dormancy that lasted as long as it took for the Great Rains to enable their instinctive migration back to the capital hatching pools. There was such anticipation for the arrival of wetuedin. Elenn tried not to analyze her own lack of excitement. She loosened and wrestled another heavy block from its position and threw it behind her.

The command to rotate was made with a whistle and Elenn moved with two other guards from the capital wall to the bank of the stream. Looking down, she could see where the build-up of blocks had effectively anchored the softer ground in place. The efforts continued. As blocks were set behind her, Elenn, taking cues from Henik, dropped them over the side slightly further down.

She was turning around to pick up another block when she felt her footing slip. For a second she tried to catch herself, thinking she had just slipped in the mud, but with a shocking realization, she saw that the whole section of ground under her feet was collapsing into the stream. The last thing she caught out of her eye was a slice of ground with layers of dryer crumbly soil underneath. Jolting cold and the swiftness of the current overtook her awareness. She reached up but there was nothing to grasp, and the rush of water swallowed her before she could even fill her lungs with air.

She felt herself being carried like a rag with the force of the muddy water, so opaque that she could not tell which way to move in order to get air. Her back banged against one of the blocks from the wall, and her shoulder scraped against mud. The current threw her against the opposite side of the retaining wall, and she got a momentary glimpse of rain pouring from the sky and caught a quick gulp of air. She hit her head against rock. The impact was dizzying but she remained conscious. Instinctively she pulled her hands up to her head to guard it from another collision. Her raised arms bounced against more rocks. She managed to grab a corner of rock that was jutting out from the side. She held on with both hands, her head half out of the water. She turned her head away from the rush, trying to fill her lungs with air. She could see the churning water downstream.

Suddenly Elenn remembered who she was and made a connection. This would be a perfect way to die. It would be seen as a valorous death, and no one would ever have to know that she was barren. All she had to do was let go of the rock. What reason was there to hold on? If she lived, what would come later? She would get sicker, become like that barren in the lichen field. Eventually she would die without a passing. Until then, there would be only waiting for the inevitable. And when would that come? *When will I go? No matter, It is not soon enough!*

Let go! Let go! Why wouldn't her arms obey her?

"MASTER ELENN! MASTER ELENN! HOLD ON!" It was Deben.

Let go! This is your chance!

"WE'RE THROWING YOU A ROPE!"

It was going to be too late. She couldn't let go now. They were all there to help her, to save her ... from what? for what?

A rope fell across the rock she was clutching. She took it with one hand, then the other, letting go of the rock. The water dragged her quickly to the side of the stream bank, where the guards pulled her out.

She came out stumbling and coughing in the downpour. Her rain cape was swept away, but she was not seriously injured. She looked up and saw Henik and the guards standing around her. Water was pouring off the hoods of their capes in little streams. She was bent over, catching her breath.

"Are you all right?" shouted Henik.

"Yes ..."

"Are you sure?" she yelled.

"I'm all right," answered Elenn. The drumming of the rain continued. She looked up and saw the hesitation on Henik's face. Apparently she didn't look all right. She straightened up and put on a brave smile. *"It was just a bit of a scare!"* she

yelled through the rainfall. Henik didn't need to know that she was thinking about having missed her opportunity to die.

Henik nodded reassuringly. *"Just sit here for now and catch your breath!"* she answered. *"I'm sending you back! You must keep warm and get rest! We'll have enough hands—some of the guards from Central are on their way to help! If you're ready, you can come back in the morning!"* She shouted something to Deben. Deben turned to Elenn.

"Come on!" shouted Deben, *"I'm taking you back to the station!"*

Elenn was unsteady on her feet. She was badly bruised and had some cuts on her head and legs. Deben led her back the way they had come and through the northgate, then through small side streets in a shortcut back to Quarterhouse. Elenn followed silently. She felt slightly embarrassed about needing to be rescued.

The streets of the capital rushed with water. Uedin stood under awnings and looked out windows into the falling rain, a look of celebration on their faces. Some were in the flooded streets, sloshing through the rain with bundles of food and drink to visit acquaintances. She heard singing in a few buildings. It was a new novade.

They finally reached the Flatpools District, and Deben took Elenn into the guards' residence.

"Are the rest of you going to work all night?" asked Elenn.

"No, we'll be back in a few hours. The rain's already slackening up a bit—by morning the current will already be going down. That one spot collapsed, but we shouldn't have any more problems now that the rain is slowing down."

"I'll be ready to work again by morning."

"Don't worry about it. See how you feel. We're glad you didn't drown." Deben looked at her seriously.

Elenn said nothing. She made a gesture of gratitude as Deben went out.

Later, with a blanket wrapped around her and a bowl of hot porridge in front of her, Elenn closed her eyes and listened to the rush of water in the gutters outside and the incessant pounding of rain on the roof. She swallowed a mouthful. The act of eating felt like a concession of failure.

For the next few years, Elenn would think back often on the moment when she had come close to letting go of her life. She would picture herself clinging to the rock with the torrent dragging at her. Her grasp on the rock had been the only thing that had committed her to a life she did not desire to live out. What had stopped her from taking advantage of the opportunity to escape the indignity of a barren life? Was it courage or cowardice? Many were the times that she would sadly recall the fateful moment and suspect that it had been the latter.

Wetuedins' Descent

It was five days into the Great Rains. The rain had decreased to a drizzle. Wetuedin had been spotted in a few of the hatching pools. Elenn found the following message waiting for her at the guard station.

> *Invitation to Master Elenn, Flatpools District Guard.*
>
> *Quarterhouse tutors and caretakers will celebrate the New Novade and arrival of wetuedin on the first evening of the greater moon's quarter. Former advisees are asked to attend. Please bring song or verse for sharing.*
>
> *Lern Beyan kiman kiman uedin olor.*
>
> *Teaching Master Domas, Quarterhouse*

There were two other new guards who had come from Quarterhouse. She hadn't met either of them before joining the guards. They were enthusiastic trainees—no doubt the guards had always been their first choice of assignment. It would probably be best if the three of them went to the celebration together. She turned the invitation over and admired the Quarterhouse emblem on the paper.

"Master Elenn, you're dripping water on the station floor!" Master Deben scolded teasingly. Elenn had been working with Deben for the past two days. Some of the streets had become impassable with mud, and the foot traffic had to be temporarily redirected while gravel and straw were brought in. Elenn found it hard to get used to interacting casually with older generation masters.

"Pardon me Master Deben," responded Elenn seriously. "I'll mop it."

"No need to mop it, I'm not being serious," said Deben. "There's no keeping the floor clean at a time like this with the guards in and out all day." So it had been friendly teasing. Elenn laughed nervously.

"Oh, I see you got your message—good." She was slurping a cup of steaming milkgrass tea.

"It's an invitation to join the Quarterhouse masters for a celebration of new novade and wetuedin's coming."

"Have you seen any of the wetuedin yet? They're beautiful." Deben refilled her cup from a small pot and offered some to Elenn. Elenn politely declined.

"Not yet," said Elenn. "The water's still too muddy—I can't see anything in there." She folded up the message and put it in her sleeve.

"Well, you'll probably see some in the flatpools if you go to the Quarterhouse celebration. They say the sediment settles quickly there. I'm not from the Quarterhouse myself, but I remember hearing about it from other guards."

"Which house did you come from, Master Deben?"

"Whiteroof." Whiteroof wasn't known for verse or scholarship. The Whiteroof masters were pragmatists. They produced a few architects, but mostly trained their unnamed in carpentry, metal work and the like. It made sense that Deben came to the guards from Whiteroof. To have come to the guards from the Quarterhouse, where the unnamed were schooled in history and poetry, was a little more peculiar. "Masters Hela and Simol have already requested duty suspension on the first. Shall I process a request for you as well?"

"Yes, thank you, Master Deben." In many ways Elenn missed the world of ideas and poetic sensibilities that reigned at Quarterhouse. This celebration might be one of her last visits back for a while. They wanted the alumni to bring verses or songs. Sometimes on such occasions the masters would compose originals right at the flatpools. She wondered whether it would be better to find an obscure poem to recite or compose something there.

"Oh, by the way, Master Elenn, a representative from the infirmary was here earlier. They're starting testing for barren syndrome soon. Apparently they've decided to begin with the second generation masters."

Elenn felt a draining sensation as she received the news, but she did her best to appear unfazed. "Is there anything we need to know?" she asked.

Deben must have noticed something in Elenn's voice or composure, because she looked at her and hesitated before she answered. "The medic said they would extract a small bit of skullsap with a needle." She tapped the back of her neck. "They'll probably test the third and fourth generation later on."

"When will this be?" asked Elenn.

"Sometime in the next shorter moon cycle, I believe," answered Deben. She looked earnestly at Elenn. "Are you concerned about the test, Master Elenn?" Elenn didn't answer.

Deben lowered her voice. "Master Elenn, you are not barren! I've been around the barren enough to recognize them." Elenn was moved by Deben's firmness and decency. "You will see," Deben continued, "As I consider it more, I am convinced that this test for barren syndrome is going to be a good thing. There are probably many like you who have gotten it in your heads that you're barren. The test will tell you once and for all."

Elenn felt the kindness and good intentions in Deben's words. She closed her eyes and held both hands over her mouth to express her gratitude.

On the night of the Quarterhouse New Novade's celebration, Elenn met Hela and Simol, the other two trainees who had come from Quarterhouse. The two of them had known each other since days after Namesgiving and had joined the guards together. On the way to Quarterhouse, Hela and Simol talked happily about their assignments. They made a courteous effort to include Elenn in the conversation as they walked through the muddy streets. The rain had stopped that afternoon, at least for a while.

"What about you Master Elenn, are you doing a poem or a song for the masters?" asked Hela.

"I haven't chosen anything, so I suppose I'll compose a poem right at the flatpools deck," she answered.

"Oh. That can be very difficult," said Hela a bit sarcastically. "Master Simol is going to do that too—she's been working on it for days!" It was a joke that only Quarterhouse-trained masters would appreciate. The verse-writing parties—for snow, stars, whatever—were supposed to involve spontaneous writing. There would always be some namely ones and show-offs who couldn't resist figuring out poems in their heads well in advance so that they would have something impressive to share.

"Don't believe her, Master Elenn!" said Simol with mock indignation. "She's just jealous because she's not capable of anything more than a yeast-drinking song!" Elenn liked these two guard masters with whom she had Quarterhouse upbringing in common, but she had already established a reputation for herself as being quiet and withdrawn. She allowed them to go ahead and think of her as having nothing to say.

It was just getting dark when they entered the familiar Quarterhouse compound. They all felt strange to be coming there as guests. The masters were gathering at the granary and observation deck over the flatpools. There were young masters from many assignments around the capital. The Quarterhouse masters did indeed have yeastdrink. They were serving it warm. Elenn accepted a cup. Master Domas recognized her and crossed the hall to welcome her.

"Master Domas, good to see you!" It had been less than a year since Elenn had left the Quarterhouse, but Domas seemed much older, smaller than when Elenn had spoken with her last.

"Young Master Elenn! I think of you so often! How is it going with the guards?"

"Just fine, Master Domas. They're very decent masters. Unnamely."

"Well I'm glad to hear you're doing well. I was afraid I let you down by not encouraging you to enter the temple."

"Please don't think that. I would not have been at home with the servers. I prefer an ordinary life with the masters."

Domas seemed pleased with this answer. "You are one of us, aren't you! All right then, come and have some yeastdrink. The caretaker masters made oilcakes! And you've got to have some lichen soup—last summer gave us a beautiful crop, wait till you try it." Domas was so informal and familiar-acting. It made Elenn uncomfortable. Was it because Domas was aging quickly, or was it just that she no longer possessed the authority of a tutor now that Elenn was a master herself? She didn't know, but when Domas excused herself and went to laugh and talk about old times with some of the other Ro masters, Elenn was rather relieved.

She sampled the food and drink that the caretakers had prepared. She exchanged greetings and niceties with some of her former tutors. Master Hera announced that everyone should move out onto the observation deck to view the wetuedin. Elenn followed the crowd.

One of the apprentice caretakers lit a lamp and put it on the end of a long pole. She put it into a holder so that it extended over the surface of the flatpool below the deck. The masters were leaning over the rail of the observation deck looking down.

"There! There's one!" one of them shouted.

"Oh!" The older masters voiced their giddy excitement without embarrassment.

The caretaker lit a second and then a third lamp, so that the surface of the pool was illuminated. The water was too murky to see anything swimming in it, but occasionally a small creature, fishlike but with a bulbous head, would splash at the surface. Another caretaker brought a bowl of grain and tossed it out. This resulted in a considerable splashing on the surface as fifteen or twenty wetuedin converged to feed. The masters jumped and shouted with delight.

There were tables with paper and coalsticks for masters who wanted to compose poems right there on the deck. Elenn stood alone and gazed at the surface of the flatpool before looking for a table to write.

It was unimaginable that she had once been a wetuedin herself, maybe even there in the spot she was looking at. Her earliest memory was of Master Inip, gone now to her own passing. Elenn remembered the soft fabric of Master Inip's robe brushing against her as the master leaned across the table to ladle salted porridge into the unnameds' little bowls. Elenn had loved that salted porridge. One of the wetuedin in the pool below her could be the spawn of Master Inip.

There was a table open on the end. Elenn looked around to make sure that no other master was waiting, and then took the position. She wrote the poem in one draft, folded it and put it in her sleeve.

The recital of songs and verses lasted well into the night. Each master made a formal self introduction before reciting her piece. Hela did sing a song for masters. Not a yeastdrinking song, but an ode to the Quarterhouse written by a capital administrator during the Claybridge Period. It was well received. Simol had written a short verse.

> *Songs and verses in the hundreds*
> *Stories told by tutors and caretakers*
> *All easily put away*
> *When eyes behold the shimmering wetuedin*
> *for the first time.*

Not bad at all, thought Elenn. It seemed to express a spontaneous sentiment. If Simol had written it in advance, she had certainly anticipated the experience cleverly.

The older masters laughed when Benar recited a parody of one of the senior tutor's poems from the celebration that took place one novade ago. Elenn was amazed that so many of them remembered it.

When it was time to read her piece, Elenn felt surprisingly at ease. She rose and stepped to the front of the assembly and spoke calmly.

"I am newly-named Elenn, second generation master, new in training with the capital guard masters, Flatpools District." As she spoke she looked out and saw many of her former tutors and caretakers looking on with encouraging faces. There was Master Leksa, Master Domas, Master Udow and Master Benar. Elenn continued, "With a grateful heart to the Quarterhouse masters for raising me and teaching me in the ways of uedin life, I offer this poem in honor of the new novade and the arrival of the wetuedin." And then she read her poem.

> *The silty milk in which you swim*
> *I know has carried you here from a lake*
> *Where is the lake from whose waters you've come?*
> *Tell me about that lake, so far away.*
> *Tell me by your swimming and skipping on the*
>   *pool.*
> *Tell me by your tail-flittering and glimmering.*
> *Tell me, and perhaps I will dream about it.*

The assembled nodded silently in acknowledgment of Elenn's poetry. Elenn noticed a ro-uedin, one she did not know, with a wistful look in her eye; perhaps her mind was very much on her own passing. Even if everyone else was only being polite, that one seemed to have been moved, and that was enough.

Later Master Udow found Elenn and complimented her. "It seems very far away when you're young," said Udow, her eyes pink from too much yeastdrink. "But before you know it, you're old like me, and your pilgrimage will be right around the corner!" Elenn smiled and nodded, though she wondered if Lake Ceulan was something she would ever see.

The Testing

A combined moon cycle had passed since the rains had stopped. Elenn awoke to the sound of birdsong and the brilliance of sunshine coming in the window of the guards' residence. She pushed herself up from her matting and looked around. It must be late, she thought. Most of the guards were gone, their mattings put away. She put on her guard's robe and folded up her own matting.

Later, after a cup of yam gruel in the meal hall, she checked in at the guard station before heading out to Crafting District. She was working with a team up there to check the roof thatching of all the buildings for noxious mold.

The guard assigned to clerk duty looked up momentarily from a grid she was working on. "Oh, Master Elenn. Master Henik wants you to stay at the station today."

"Oh really? I've been working with the team up in Crafting."

"You might be sent to join them later, but you and the other second-generation guards are getting physical exams today. Master Henik said you could occupy yourself around the residence until the medics arrive." The guard master doing clerk duty continued to study the grid as she said this.

"Did Master Henik leave specific instructions—chores or anything?" asked Elenn.

"She didn't, but I think the other five are plowing a small area out back while the soil is still soft. Master Wanba thinks onions will grow well back there. If you don't have anything else to do, you could go help them." Elenn got some work gloves and went to help the others.

As she rounded the corner, she heard them singing. They were singing while waiting to get tested for barren syndrome! It must be in an effort to cover up their nervousness with bravado, she thought. Then she realized that they weren't really singing. They were reciting the Names of the Lern. Elenn didn't expect the guards ever to do such a thing ... but why not? They were uedin like her. But did they know that one wasn't supposed to draw the attention of Lern Beyana without a calm mind? She looked at their faces. They looked calm enough—sober with the agenda of the day, but calm.

Lehera Beyana Yana Ya ..." the leader sang out.

"*Lehera Beyana Yana Ya ...*" they repeated in chorus.

"*Lerna Beyana ulrana uedina ...*"

"*Lerna Beyana ulrana uedina ...*" Elenn joined in and bent down to start picking rocks out of the freshly plowed dirt.

It was a consolation to give herself over to the familiar chants, and it stopped the mind's spiraling. Besides, knowing that the guards even *wanted* to chant the names of Lern Beyana gave Elenn a very good feeling. It made her feel that she wasn't so alone. Even if they were all on the brink of learning who was and who wasn't barren, they had some tender element of uedin identity in common. The air was fresh and moist. The sunlight was warm on her back.

They worked through the morning. Near mid-day, Simol had just offered to go prepare a simple meal for them when the guard on clerk duty came around the corner.

"The medic is here. She'll see you all in the station after you wash."

The young guards rested their gardening tools against a rail and silently headed to the washroom. Elenn followed in the back and washed the dirt off her hands when the others were finished. Two ro-uedin medics were talking when they entered the station. They looked up.

"Are you all here?"

"Yes." It was Hela who answered. "There are only six of us second-generation masters in this station."

The ro-uedin made a notation and looked up to introduce herself. "I am Ferin, and this is Master Goril. You understand the masters council has asked us to test for barren syndrome. We know that this may be hard for you, and we appreciate your cooperation."

The other medic, Goril, spoke. "We want you to know that our results are not intended to be used against any of you. If we find that there are barren uedin among you, we'll be doing all we can to help them. We'll know the results in a few days." She looked at each of them with honest concern. Then she added sadly, "We've already found two barren second-generation masters among our own apprentice medics at the infirmary."

After a pause, Goril continued. "The test involves taking a drop of skullsap from the umbilical artery on the back of the neck. We can determine in the infirmary lab how the skullsap is being metabolized. That's how we identify barren syndrome. If you're found to have barren syndrome, it could be years before you develop symptoms. We may be able to treat the symptoms more effectively with time. So even if you are found to be barren, you shouldn't give up hope. Are there any questions, masters?"

None of them had any. The medics had them come one at a time to sit on a stool. Master Goril took the skullsap samples by using a tiny knife and a small pad to collect a drop of the skullsap from the back of their necks and then put a small bandage on the spot. Master Ferin put each pad in a separate sheet of oil paper, folded it up, and attached it to a tag that she marked with name, date and location.

On her way out, Elenn asked the guard on clerk duty, "Shall I report to Crafting District now to help the team that's checking for mold in the roof thatchings?"

"It's not necessary. Master Henik sent word that you could all take the rest of the day for personal needs." Elenn left the station.

Personal needs? Elenn sighed deeply. She had not really thought much about how the medics were going to administer their test. She now wished they had called the guards in one at a time instead of letting them all stand around like that. It wasn't the test itself that Elenn had found disturbing—she had had plenty of time to prepare for the fact. But Elenn did not anticipate the strange sensation she had when she saw Master Ferin make the little incision to the back of the other guards' necks.

She walked back to the place where they were preparing the ground for the onion patch. There was only one guard there. She was collecting the gardening tools to put them away.

"Oh, Master Elenn," she said. "I guess that wasn't so bad, was it?" It was Nemis. Elenn didn't know her very well, and wasn't even sure which domicile she had come from.

"Are we going to do any more work here?" asked Elenn.

"Not today. The rest of us are going to take food and walk out to the canyon for the afternoon. Come with us."

"Thank you, Master Nemis," said Elenn, "but I'm going to stay in the residence. Please pass on my regrets to the others." As she said it, Deben came around the corner behind her. She was overhearing the conversation.

"Master Elenn," said Deben, "I think it would be very good if you would go along with Master Nemis and the others." She looked sternly at Elenn. "Go on, both of you. I'll put away your gardening tools. Master Wanba will be very pleased with your progress on her onion patch. Now go along."

Elenn raised one hand to her mouth to express thanks and followed Nemis. It was a beautiful day, and since they were a longer moon cycle past the Great Rains, there would probably be many plants budding and flowering in the canyon.

Results

The next night, Elenn was washing out pots and kettles in the residence kitchen when Simol entered. "Master Elenn," she said, "I'm supposed to take over for you. You're needed in the station." Elenn dried her hands and put on her guards robe.

When she got inside the station, there was only one lamp lit, and no one was there but Deben. Deben was standing and staring at a calligraphy scroll hanging on the wall which said, *"A uedin's best effort is her purest exercise."* It was done in a guard's hand and wasn't very artistic.

"Master Deben, you called for me," said Elenn.

"Yes." Deben turned around but she didn't look directly at Elenn. She looked toward the ceiling as if preparing to make some sort of official statement of guard policy.

"Can I help you with anything, Master Deben?" asked Elenn.

"Master Elenn …" she hesitated and then spoke with efficiency. "I obtained the results from yesterday's procedure." Elenn was not expecting this so soon.

"I thought Master Ferin said it would take a few days …" started Elenn. She was perplexed.

"I have a few good friends at the infirmary." explained Deben. "I asked them to inform me early of any troubling results."

Troubling results. Elenn understood what she was being told.

"Master Elenn, I will do everything I can to help you."

Elenn listened calmly. So it was definite. Well, how could it have been otherwise? Elenn had sometimes wondered what it would mean if she had been wrong about herself all this time. Would she then have gradually shifted back into normal thinking and attitudes? She had worried that even if she weren't barren, she was damaged just by thinking for so long that she was. At any rate, that possibility no longer existed. Elenn was barren. She understood what it meant for her.

Deben herself was clearly distraught with the news, maybe because she had been wrong with her reassurances. Elenn knew that the courteous thing to do would be to tell her that she needn't feel bad because her intentions had been good. But she didn't have the strength to concern herself with Deben. Her mind could only contain one thing at this moment, and it was her own fate.

Deben spoke quietly. "I don't understand how you could have possibly known of your own condition, Master Elenn. The day I found you in the library, I understand that you had had some kind of very disturbing dream. But bad dreams are usually just signs of stress and anxiety."

Elenn wasn't sure how to answer. She responded slowly. "Before I had the dream, I think I knew deep inside that there was something wrong with me, I just didn't know what it was. I just knew that I wasn't like most of the other child-uedin. I worried. I worried about being namely, about being good at the exercises, all sorts of things. I worried despite not having an obvious reason to worry. When I had that dream, it made sense to me. Of course I needed to worry. I was barren." Elenn was looking down at the floor as she spoke. She knew that her explanation was not anything that would make Deben understand any better, but it didn't matter. She went on. "I hoped that I might be wrong. I wanted to believe you when you told me that it was common to develop such fears in stressful times. But I wasn't wrong, was I, Master Deben?"

Deben knew that her past attempts to reassure Elenn had been in vain. There could be no more false reassurances. "No you weren't, Master Elenn. You were correct," she answered sadly.

"What will happen now?" asked Elenn.

"I don't know exactly, but I will try to arrange for you to stay with us as long as you are able." said Deben. Then she asked, "Do you feel any … different—yet?"

Elenn thought about this. "I feel very different. Hopelessly different." Deben didn't say anything. She waited for Elenn to finish explaining herself. "I don't know what symptoms a uedin with barren syndrome is expected to have. For me, it's mostly in my own feelings that I am on a different path from normal uedin."

"We will probably hear something from Master Ferin in the next day or two. At least you know that the master medics will help you however they can."

"Were there any others among us who tested as barren?"

"No, Master Elenn. You're the only one who tested as barren among the second-generation guards." She looked as though she wanted say more, but she remained silent.

Elenn nodded and looked at the floor. "Good. That's good news."

"And by the way, I'm not planning to tell any of the guards about this. Master Wanba will be receiving a copy of the official report from the medics. I don't know if she'll tell Henik and the other senior guards, but I'm sure there will be nothing said to the younger guards. There's no reason for you to tell them about it either."

Elenn accepted this as direction. She made a farewell gesture and walked out the door.

That night Elenn dreamt again that she was a bodiless spirit flying away from the capital. She came to a lake in the hills and found an area where the shore was littered with crumbling bones. There was a ro-uedin there, kneeling at the water's edge for her passing-of-life. A golden glow poured out the ro-uedin's skullwomb as she began to give birth. It was the life force, transferring from ro-uedin to spawn. Seeing this, Elenn descended and drew close to the ro-uedin. When she was close enough, she was hopelessly compelled to sip at the fluid light. Finding it irresistible, she drank deeply, feeling the life force restore her own aching emptiness. When she finished, she looked at the face of the ro-uedin. It was Master Domas, but she was dead, as were the contents of her skullwomb. Master Domas lay there on a bed of bones, a look of horror fixed on her face from the realization that her passing had been stolen from her. Elenn woke immediately after having this dream, and tried to understand what it might mean. Master Domas was probably the uedin that she admired most in all the capital, and Elenn had dreamt that she had destroyed her.

Two days later the guards were retrieving blocks from the bottom of the stream gulley to restore the section of capital wall that they had dismantled during the Great Rains. The second generation guards were all there working on it when a messenger came. She called Simol first to report to the station. They all knew she was being called in to get her results from the testing for barren syndrome.

Simol's gait was shaky as she followed the messenger away from the work site. She was clearly terrified of the results. Elenn found herself feeling resentment toward her fellow guard masters. She imagined herself shouting out, "Don't worry Master Simol—don't worry any of you! I'm the only one here who is barren. You can all go celebrate your good health." Simol returned later in the morning smiling and relieved. Elenn kept quiet as the others were called away one by one.

Elenn was finally called in the afternoon. She felt weak and tired as she walked behind the messenger, but there was no more anxiety. She was grateful to Deben for informing her of her result in advance. In the station hall, Wanba, dressed in her senior guard's garb, was seated at the table with Ferin and

Goril, the same medic masters who had administered the second-generation guards their tests.

"Master Elenn, please join us at the table here. You remember Master Ferin and Master Goril from the infirmary laboratory," said Wanba.

"Yes, Master Wanba." Elenn made polite gestures of greeting to the guests.

Goril spoke first. "Master Elenn, thank you for your cooperation in the testing. As you know, the masters council decided that we can deal most practically and sensitively with the barren crisis if we know how many of our young uedin are affected. We've tested about two hundred of the second generation, which means the testing of your generation is about halfway complete. The results we have so far are not good. We suspected an incidence rate of four or five percent. Unfortunately, we have already found thirty-seven cases of barren syndrome, which means the rate may be as high as nine percent."

So this is how they go about breaking the news, thought Elenn. They are too uncomfortable to just say what the result is.

Ferin took over. "Master Elenn, we are confident that we can make accommodations for uedin with barren syndrome that will minimize the harm both for themselves and the rest of the capital." She took a deep breath and spoke in a plain and calm voice. "We're sorry to inform you that your test has indicated that you are among the afflicted. We will be working closely with you to monitor the condition and help you as much as we can." They all looked to watch Elenn's response.

The medic masters were prepared to see an emotional breakdown. However, Elenn sat still and said nothing.

Master Wanba began asking questions on Elenn's behalf, partly to help the meeting progress smoothly. "Can you tell us, Master Ferin and Master Goril, is there any better knowledge of this condition that will help us understand what we are dealing with?" Elenn knew Wanba was trying to be helpful by facilitating, but she felt nothing but disdain for this posturing. Wanba had been sitting with these medics all afternoon—surely she had already heard whatever there was to know.

"Well, obviously, there is the simple fact that a barren uedin has no embryo and is never going to reproduce." Goril spoke coolly as if she were addressing a group of apprentice medics. "This in itself presents a terrible burden to the barren individual. Unfortunately, there are other physical problems that come up. We are beginning to understand that the deterioration of the barren's mental and physical health are associated with the fact that the body continues to produce skullsap. Without an embryo, the sap cannot be metabolized properly. The body reabsorbs it, but the resulting side effects include physical overdevelopment and gradual derangement."

Elenn let her eyes wander, following the cracks between the stone slabs on the floor. She looked around at the undecorated woven wall covering and work tables stacked with documents and reference texts, trying to distract herself. She knew that what she was hearing was important, but she didn't want to listen. She wanted to run somewhere outside of the capital and forget everything. She longed for the days before she had a name, before she knew what she was. Master Wanba kept looking at her with expectations as if she thought Elenn should show more interest, ask questions and nod enthusiastically just to be polite. But she couldn't bring herself to play along.

"Will Master Elenn need to adopt any special regimen to deal with her particular health needs?"

"We will work closely with you, Master Elenn. What we can offer you is our dedication to helping you as much as we possibly can. That includes providing you with treatment for physical side effects as they arise and individual support to help you gradually come to terms with your condition."

What support could they possibly offer? Elenn felt hopeless about it, but she decided it would do no harm to ask them directly. She thought she would be able to ask the simple question without betraying the emotional burden she felt, but when she opened her mouth to speak, her voice cracked with emotion.

"How can you possibly support me in coming to terms with my... condition?"

The air was heavy as the senior guard and the two medics registered the depth of the young guard's despair. They knew their help was meager and insufficient. But even if there was next to nothing they could do, they must commit to doing all they could. This young uedin was one of many who would need their help.

Goril, who had spoken with the distance of expertise, responded with a note of sympathy in her voice that provided Elenn a small bit of consolation. "Master Elenn, admittedly there is little we can do. The council has asked the caretaker masters for volunteers to form a small corps of helpers for the barren. Already some of them have responded that they wish to accept this role."

Elenn listened to this. The caretakers were trained and dedicated to the care of the child-uedin. As the unnamed grew and matured, the role of caretakers became less important. There was something humiliating about having to rely upon them once again in adulthood. But even as Elenn felt a tinge of insult around this arrangement, she also understood the sacrifice that the caretakers were making by leaving the comfort and satisfaction of their role with the unnamed to work with the barren. It was not something she could look upon without gratitude.

"Master Wanba, Master Goril, Master Ferin," she said, momentarily looking at each of them with respect and then raising hands to face in humility, "thank you for your help and your kindness. I will cooperate in every way I can." She looked down now into her folded hands, which rested just below her lips. Yes, this was the proper response. Elenn felt the strange sensation of a temporary reconciliation that shallowly blankets a deep ill, like the crust of an oilcake gone bad, one that looks fine and hides the rancidness within.

Incident at the Flatpools

Deben was awakened from a deep sleep by the sound of clappers. It was the emergency alarm. She jumped into her garb, stepped into her boots and sprang for the station. Two of the junior guards were already there receiving a report from someone wearing a robe from Quarterhouse.

"What's happening?" asked Deben.

"The flatpools at Quarterhouse," huffed the young caretaker, "There's been an intrusion!"

Deben looked around to see if the six guards on duty were all there yet. There were only four. Who was missing? She pushed aside the door tarp to look at the assignment board on the wall. Nemis and Simol had been there to receive the report. Ribol and Hela were there. Ippal wasn't there yet... And Elenn. Elenn was missing. She brushed the thought from her mind and turned back to the Quarterhouse master.

"What was it? Animal?"

"We don't know—we didn't see." The caretaker was in anguish. "But one of the wetuedin is dead." She seemed ashamed to report what they had found. "Only its head was eaten. The rest of the body was left on the rocks."

They all knew what it meant, but none of them said anything. It was the killing pattern of the barren. Deben looked back toward the guards residence hoping to see Elenn coming, but there was nothing in that direction but the shadow of tall grass blowing slightly in the breeze. She didn't want to allow the thought in her mind to take hold. Even if Elenn was barren, she was only a second-generation uedin. It was much too early for her to have one of those fits of madness that the barren were known to have.

"Where are Master Elenn and Master Ippal?" she finally asked to see whether the other guards might know.

"Inside," said Simol, "getting tar oil and torches." Deben felt a wave of relief at this bit of information. She dashed inside to find Henik with Elenn and Ippal. They were all working quickly to tie oil-soaked rags around torches, which would be needed in the dark since both moons were new.

"Master Deben—do you realize nobody ever told the trainees where we keep the tar oil? Master Elenn and Master Ippal were here first, but they couldn't prepare the torches because they didn't know where the tar oil was stored." Henik looked sternly at Deben to convey her displeasure.

"I am responsible for the oversight, Master Henik," said Deben with a gesture of apology. "Is everything ready now?" She was so glad to find Elenn inside the station that Henik's scolding hardly fazed her. She was wearing a smile of relief when Elenn looked up from her task. Elenn looked back, caught her smiling, and responded with a look of bewilderment.

"What did the Quarterhouse master say?" asked Henik.

Deben then realized that Henik and the trainees didn't yet know what was happening. She noticed that Elenn was watching her to see if what she had to say would explain the peculiar smile.

"Apparently there's been an intrusion at Quarterhouse—in the flatpools."

Elenn's mind took a moment before making any connection. Intrusion at the flatpools... some barren uedin probably involved. And Deben was smiling about it. Why? Then it hit her. Deben was glad to see that Elenn was there because she had been afraid that Elenn might have been the intruder. But this was an emergency and there was no time to think about herself. She disregarded her thoughts and picked up four of the torches to carry outside.

"Someone needs to stay at the station," said Deben, looking at Elenn. This time, Elenn stared back at Deben with plain resentment. She felt insulted, but she said nothing. Deben saw that she was being misunderstood. She only wanted to protect Elenn. It would do her no good to see the dead wetuedin killed by a barren, or worse yet to confront the responsible deranged barren if they should find her somewhere in the capital.

Henik looked at Deben with even more displeasure. "Master Deben, *you* will stay." Henik was a senior guard, so there could be no discussion. Elenn and Ippal hurried out with the torches. As Henik passed Deben, she looked at her with great seriousness and said, "I don't know how you know what you know, Master Deben. But we have no intention of denying Master Elenn any of the full responsibility of her position as guard master until it becomes necessary to do otherwise. Do you understand?"

"Yes Master Henik." said Deben. She remained with her hands at her face in humility and obedience as Henik passed her and walked out. She heard some brief instructions being given and then listened to the sound of the guards running off in the direction of the Quarterhouse. Then she brought her hands down and looked around the station. On the floor there were still containers and supplies that the trainees had taken out when they were searching for tar oil. She slowly occupied herself putting everything back. She understood that she had been negligent and mistaken. She had failed to provide the trainees with proper review of emergency supplies, and she had furthermore created a crisis of confidence by trying to protect Master Elenn from the inevitable. But there was something in the young uedin that moved her very deeply. It didn't seem enough to trust in the regular goodwill of the capital. She felt that it was not going to be much help for poor Master Elenn.

The guards reached Quarterhouse within minutes. They found a small congregation standing together in silence on the observation deck. Henik spoke to the Quarterhouse masters and then returned to the other guards. They stood at attention for instructions.

"None of the masters actually saw what happened here, but it's obvious that the wetuedin was caught and killed by a barren. They've already observed the body. It was beat against rocks. I need two of you—Ribol and Elenn—you'll stay here with me to investigate and take care of the body. Simol, you will return to the station and wake the off-duty guards. Give a report to Master Wanba and help her organize a search. Master Ippal, send messengers to Northgate and Central stations, letting them know that a barren has killed a wetuedin at Quarterhouse and is on the loose. Hela, you'll be guarding the hatching pool over at Whiteroof for the rest of the night. Nemis, you go to the hatching pool at Bramble and keep watch there."

The guard masters quickly dispersed to carry out Henik's orders. Ribol, an older guard master who had never pursued rank, stayed behind with Elenn to assist Henik.

"What's the easiest way down to the rocks?" called Henik to the Quarterhouse masters who were still standing on the observation deck in silence, not knowing what to do.

"Come this way, Master." A young caretaker master whom Elenn did not recognize led them to the granary at the back end of the observation deck. It had a back doorway that opened to a rickety stairway down to the rocks that bordered the flatpool.

"Would the barren have come through here?" asked Ribol.

"No," answered Henik. "Barren are very strong—especially when they have an attack of derangement. I'm sure she easily climbed directly over any obstacles and jumped right into the flatpool." She spoke of the barren plainly and without reservation, even though she knew her remarks were bound to have a special impact on Elenn.

The body of the wetuedin was still lying on the rocks. The guards and the caretaker master approached it with a mixture of horror and respect. Ribol held her torch down to provide light. They looked at the silvery white body of the dead wetuedin. Neither Elenn nor the others had ever seen the body of a wetuedin up close before. It was plump and tiny at the same time, with very clear preindications of its uedin body to come. The tail was translucent so that it was easy to imagine it eventually coming off. The small appendages had the shape of shortened uedin arms and legs with little hands and feet encased in webbing. The arms of this poor dead creature had been brutally broken. Most shocking was what remained of the wetuedin's head. It had been first beaten unconscious and then some sort of tool used to break open its head from the back. A good portion of its face remained, and even in its undeveloped state it held a wincing expression that was hauntingly uedin.

"Shield the Lern …" Ribol uttered quietly. She bowed her head and put her hands over her eyes. They all paused to take in the magnitude of the tragedy. It was understood that the death of one wetuedin was not only the loss of one individual life, but the end of a singular lineage that had survived countless generations.

Henik tried to sustain the attitude of guard service, but there were disturbed tones in her voice as she spoke. "I would guess that the intruder caught the wetuedin with her hands and killed it by holding its back appendages and swinging it against these rocks. Then she must have cut open its skull with some sort of tool."

"There were some small axes for cutting kindling for the warming stoves on the observation deck," said the caretaker master. "The barren could easily have used one of those." They looked around to see if an ax had been left on the rocks, but they concluded that whatever was used was probably pitched into the water.

"What will be the proper way to care for the body?" Henik asked the caretaker.

"Can you wait while I ask the senior masters?" she replied.

Henik nodded and the caretaker hurried up the stairway to discuss the matter with the older masters who were still standing together on the deck. Elenn heard them discussing the matter, then Henik said quietly, "Whatever they want to do with the body, Master Elenn and Master Ribol, please oblige them. I need to find Master Wanba and talk with her. The first challenge will be to find the intruder. After that there is going to be the very difficult matter of what to do with her." Elenn and Ribol nodded in obedience. Henik left them with the body and went to climb the stairway up to the deck. They stood listening to her climb the stairs and heard her expressing her condolences to the Quarterhouse masters and then excuse herself from their company.

The young caretaker master came down and spoke to Elenn and Ribol. "The Quarterhouse masters have decided to cremate the remains tomorrow under the greenbark trees behind the Quarterhouse," she said. "Would you mind carrying the body to the pavilion back there? A table is already being set up. The masters will keep vigil over the body till morning."

"Yes, certainly Master," said Ribol. Elenn noticed the deference in her speech and the humble downward gaze of her eyes. The older guards, especially those of lower rank, spoke to practically any other master with deference.

The caretaker master took both Elenn's and Ribol's guards torches, one in each hand and held them up. The body was very light, about the same as a small dog, but the two guards carried it together to show their respect. Ribol picked up from the lower abdomen just where the tail extended between the two leg-like appendages. Elenn held one hand under the neck and took hold of the broken and injured arm with her other hand.

When Elenn got that close to the body of the wetuedin, she noticed the smell. It was a strange smell, chalky and sweet. She was sure she had never smelled anything like it before, and yet it seemed strangely familiar. She had a confused sensation from having to contend with such a horrible task while finding the smell to be pleasant. It made her feel that she was connected to the evil that motivated the crime, and her stomach felt nauseous.

It was awkward to carry the dead wetuedin up the stairs together, and then all the way out of the Quarterhouse, around the back and down the earth ramp to the greenbark trees. Elenn had not been there since joining the guards, but the torch light only lit a small area. As they had been told, there was a table with lanterns there and a number of Quarterhouse masters ready to keep watch. Elenn hoped she might see Master Domas. Though she knew the dream she had had about Domas's death was only a dream, it had given her a sense of concern about Domas, and she looked forward to seeing her again. But none of the older masters were there. On the table was a clean new robe of the type that were the first given to small child-uedin. The masters had them place the body right on top of the flat unfolded robe.

Elenn and Ribol then took their torches back, spoke their final condolences, and left the Quarterhouse masters to their vigil.

"We'd better go back to the station to see whether they want us to join in the search for the barren," said Ribol.

Elenn said nothing. She wondered what they all really thought of the barren. They said nothing in hatred, but how could they not hate the barren? Elenn herself hated them, even knowing she was one of them. Her mind was spinning with the events of the past hour. She tried to banish the notion that she might someday be capable of that kind of monstrosity.

Suddenly, as she was staring into Ribol's torch-light going up the earth ramp in front of her, Elenn realized that she had unconsciously drawn her hand to her face, smelled the traces of substance on her hand and unwittingly licked her finger. The taste was like a salty, acid liquor. A shocking intoxication rushed over her. She felt her eyes bulge and blood rush to her head, hands, and feet. She stopped walking and realized what she had just done. It was not blood that Elenn had tasted on her hand. From experiences cutting her finger and so forth in her childhood, she knew that uedin blood was tasteless. This was skullsap. The sensation, instead of passing quickly, swelled and overcame her, causing her to stumble. As the torch fell from her hand, she saw, in her mind's eye, the golden flame falling in front of her again and again.

"Master Elenn! Master Elenn, are you all right?" Ribol picked up Elenn's torch and held it together with her own in one hand while she clutched Elenn by the shoulder. "Are you all right, Master Elenn?"

Elenn gathered her composure and caught her breath. But she was so stunned by what had just happened that she didn't know what to say. She only stared back into Ribol's eyes with fear and terrible shame. In her mind she felt as though she were just as guilty as the one who had killed the wetuedin. She shook her head and tried to speak, but no words came out.

Ribol continued to carry both torches in one hand and keep her other hand on Elenn's shoulder. She walked her all the way back to the station. Deben, Henik, and Wanba were inside, organizing a capital-wide search for the intruder. When they saw Elenn's face, they all assumed that Elenn was traumatized by the killing because there was a barren involved and Elenn herself had only recently learned of her own barren condition. Deben shook her head with frustration as if to say that she had known this sort of thing might happen.

"Master Elenn—" said Wanba with concern. "Oh, I was afraid of this."

"It's my fault, Master Wanba," said Henik, assessing the situation. "I was convinced that Elenn should carry out her guard assignment regardless of her personal situation. I should have been more cautious." She stopped short of telling Wanba that Deben tried to warn her, because Deben was not supposed to have knowledge of Elenn's barrenness.

Ribol had no idea what they were talking about, but she knew it was something very confidential, so she led Elenn to a seat, excused herself and left.

"Forgive me," sobbed Elenn. She didn't know exactly what she was apologizing for. Yet there seemed to be no level at which her apology was unneeded. "Please forgive me."

The sound of running feet could be heard, and then two guards appeared at the door. It was Hela and Nemis.

"Master Henik, Master Wanba, the barren is dead!" shouted Hela. Henik and Wanba looked up quizzically.

"The barren is dead! We found her at the brickyard at Whiteroof. They were firing bricks there tonight. All the kilns were going. I was on my way to the Whiteroof hatching pool, Nemis was with me, she was going to go on to Bramble, but before we got to Whiteroof, we saw the barren. We followed her, thinking that she was headed for the hatching pool, but she went right to the kilns." They all listened to Hela with puzzled faces. They were not sure what they were hearing.

"We tried to stop her, but the fire was too hot. She walked right into one of the kilns. We heard her screaming, but there was nothing we could do." Hela's face was wrinkled with anguish. "It was *horrible*."

At this point, Elenn let her head fall forward between her knees. A violent spasm shook inside her. She vomited onto her feet, mostly water and porridge from the evening's meal. She did not pick up her head, and dribbles of the vomit trickled down over her face, burning her nose and eyes.

Deben visits Benar

Hulls from the thistlebud tree were thick on the ground in front of the small hut that served as a space for caretakers to meet with the young masters with barren syndrome. Benar lived there now. She walked back and forth between the other buildings in the Quarterhouse compound for meals, supplies, and so on, but found that most of her time was spent right there in the hut. She had brought a rake from the Quarterhouse gardening shed. She was glad to have a simple chore. In the three years since the council had asked the caretaker masters to provide a volunteer corps, Benar had learned that she was of no use to any confused or suffering uedin if she did not pay careful heed to her own well-being. She consciously balanced her daily routine with a variety of activities to keep from being overwhelmed by the air of trouble and fear that came with every encounter with one of her advisees.

She still marveled at the peculiar chain of events that had led her to this role. She had never considered herself a candidate for any kind of work beyond the humble ambitions of domestic caretaker for the unnamed. All those years of washing garments, cooking, bandaging skinned knees, and telling stories, had become so predictable and comfortable that she had only imagined doing the same thing at a gradually decreasing pace until her own passing-of-life. She had been bored from time to time, wishing she had more contact with adult uedin in the capital, but that had been a fanciful interest. She certainly hadn't anticipated taking on any assignment of serious consequence.

When the corps was formed, Benar looked on from a distance with respect and appreciation as colleagues from the Quarterhouse and caretakers from Whiteroof and Bramble volunteered, but she didn't bother to even feel guilty about not volunteering herself, since it had never crossed her mind that she might be effective in the role. But there had been confusion at the beginning, and somehow word had circulated around the capital that *all* of the caretakers were going to be advising the barren, and when first one and then another young uedin arrived at her door distraught with the news of having tested positive for barren syndrome, Benar could not turn them away. They were individuals who had been raised in the Quarterhouse, and they remembered her. Even though they had been indistinguishable from each other for most of their years there, they had been fond of Benar and felt safe with her. Their trust melted any resistance she felt at first.

She raked the hulls into piles, leaving grooved trails in the dry dirt. She could hear the child-uedin playing games in the field behind the Quarterhouse. The swiftness with which the unnamed grew up was always a reminder of how quickly a novade passes, and it was hard to believe that four years had passed since the last Great Rains. Their little screams and peals of laughter in the distance had a relaxing effect on her. She sometimes regretted that she had forsaken her primary caretaker position. It was easy to keep the child-uedin happy. All they really wanted was food, warmth, and some occasional attention. The barren were another story. When she first started working with them, it had been enough simply to listen compassionately and give them simple encouragement. The ones with advanced cases of the syndrome didn't come around, even if they were assigned to specific caretakers. But things had gotten much too complicated and distressing in the course of three years. There was something wrong in the capital—the barren seemed to embody the mysterious trouble that ran like a current in uedin life, but there was more to it than the barren syndrome alone. The servers had grown so insular that they rarely sent a representative outside the temple except for major ceremonies, and then they only fulfilled their function quietly and retreated back to the temple. Certainly there were barren among the young servers—surely they had been tested. But there was never a word said about how the servers were dealing with the barren in their own community, and they certainly never came out to enlist the support of the caretakers.

Benar finished raking the thistlebud hulls into piles. When she had been a caretaker to the unnamed at Quarterhouse, she liked to use these hulls in the fire when they made smoked jelly. She planned to take the dried hulls over to the kitchen, and to see if the caretakers there could use them. She had thought there were a few large empty baskets near the hut, but she could only find one. She was only able to fit about half of the hulls into it. She would have to come back with another basket that afternoon or the wind would scatter them all over again. She tied a cover over the top of the filled basket to keep it from spilling, then fixed it to her shoulders with a strap and started toward the Quarterhouse kitchen building.

"Master Benar!"

Benar looked up to see who was calling her. It was one of the guard masters. For a minute she thought it might be Elenn—one of her advisees. Elenn only came out of duty, and usually said very little. She was always open and honest with Benar. She admitted it when she was going through periods of torment or dealing with what the medic masters referred to as "troubling impulses." But Elenn's reports were made in a spirit of cooperation. She seemed to have no expectation that Benar or any other caretaker could really help her. The first time Elenn had come, Benar thought Elenn had sought her out because she remembered her from growing up in the Quarterhouse, but it had turned out to be an appointment arranged by Master Ferin from the infirmary. Since then Elenn had always been prompt and gave full disclosure at their meetings, but Benar doubted that Elenn was benefiting from the relationship. Though Benar had even suggested that Elenn seek another caretaker to be her counselor, Elenn insisted she was quite contented to stay with her.

This wasn't Elenn, however. It was another guard master whom Benar had seen before but was not acquainted with.

"Hello, master," said Benar. "Is there something I can help you with?"

Just as she said this, one of her shoulder straps broke, the basket turned sideways, the cover came off, and all the thistlebud hulls spilled onto the ground. "Oh, how aggravating!" she muttered and took the basket off her back to refill it.

"I'm sorry—I hope I didn't startle you," said Deben. "You are Master Benar?"

"Yes I am," said Benar. "And, no, you didn't startle me. My shoulder strap broke, that's all."

"My name is Deben, and I'm a third-generation guard here in the Flatpools District. I work closely with Master Elenn." She bent to help Benar pick up the thistlebud hulls, but unlike the caretaker, she wasn't wearing gloves and the spiny shells were painful to handle.

"Oh, I see," said Benar. "I was just on my way over to the Quarterhouse. If I could just trouble you to help me pick these up, then we could walk together and discuss whatever you like."

"Yes Master Benar, thank you," said Deben. She started helping Benar pick up the hulls, handling them delicately. Benar looked at her with caution, wondering what she wanted that might have to do with Elenn. They were both quiet momentarily as they picked up hulls.

"Do you have some concerns that regard Master Elenn?" asked Benar picking up the last few. This time she didn't put the basket on her back. She just carried it in front of her. The two of them started walking slowly toward the Quarterhouse main building.

"Master Benar, I understand you have been assisting Elenn—is that true?" asked Deben.

Benar hesitated before answering, adjusting her grasp on the bulky basket. It was light but exceedingly awkward to carry. What could this guard possibly be inquiring about that wouldn't come out in the natural course of things? Had Elenn already done something that indicated derangement? "Yes, Master—" Benar halted, "I'm sorry, what was your name again, please?"

"Deben. Flatpools guards. Can I carry that for you?"

"Thank you Master Deben, but I'm fine with the basket. And you're right. I am Master Elenn's counselor through the caretaker masters' corps in service to the syndrome afflicted."

"I *do* have some concerns, Master Benar."

"I'm afraid you've come to tell me that Elenn is deteriorating. Is that the case?"

"She hasn't done anything to indicate derangement," said Deben, "but I've had many encounters with the barren since before they became numerous in the capital. I know how the syndrome progresses. Master Elenn is starting to show signs of physical enlargement. The other symptoms can't be far behind."

"Oh is that so?" Benar's voice carried both appreciation for this information and regret for its implication. "Master Deben, pardon my asking, but is your concern *on behalf* of Master Elenn, or is it in the interest of the capital?"

Deben was surprised to hear the question worded so directly, but she knew that if Benar was interested in this distinction then she could be trusted with her confidences. "My concern is absolutely on behalf of Master Elenn," she answered.

"Well then please ask me anything you like and tell me how I can help you," said Benar boldly.

"Thank you Master Benar. I believe that Elenn is already experiencing … troublesome impulses."

"The desire to consume … " Benar meant to clarify, but she didn't have polite words for it.

"Yes. I don't believe that Elenn is likely to succumb to this urge any time soon, but with time she will probably weaken."

"One of our duties in the corps is to watch that," said Benar. "We report to the medics. My understanding was that the medics communicate in turn with the guard masters when restriction becomes necessary."

"Yes, that's true. Unfortunately the events of the last year have resulted in a climate of fear. The barren are not always treated kindly when restriction becomes necessary."

"The events of last year—are you referring to the attack on Master Udow?" Benar recalled with sadness the memory of Udow's horrible death. She had come into her ecstasy and departed for final pilgrimage with much fanfare from the Quarterhouse masters. Just outside the capital wall she was attacked. Her skullwomb was crushed, its contents devoured. What was already one of the most horrible events in recent capital memory was even more disturbing to everyone because Udow survived the attack for a few days and was coherent enough to realize that her embryo had been eaten out of her head and that there would be no passing-of-life for her. She had died in anguish at the infirmary.

Deben sighed heavily at the mention of Udow. "Master Udow's end did have a terrible effect on the guards, yes. But the guards understand that the barren are not responsible for what they do when they are overtaken by derangement. It has more to do with the fact that the barren are strong and fierce. They naturally induce fear. When the guards are afraid, they become less deft in their reactions."

"That's understandable," said Benar. "But are you concerned that the guards will be too rough with Master Elenn? She is, after all, a guard herself."

"The guards all know that Master Elenn is barren. I don't know what would happen if they suddenly had to arrest her. I think they—we—are all dreading it. We want to protect Master Elenn however we can. That's why I came to you. I want you to contact me directly when Master Elenn has the first sign of derangement."

"What will you do, Master Deben?" asked Benar. They were standing in front of the Quarterhouse now. Benar put the basket on the ground at her feet.

"We will take care of her in the best way we can." said Deben. "But we need as much warning as we can possibly get. And we don't want the guards from any of the other districts to be involved."

"I understand," said Benar. "I'll stay in communication with you. Does Master Elenn know you're interested in giving her this kind of attention?"

"No, master. Please don't tell her. Master Elenn is exceedingly fair-minded, and she'll surrender to another district if she knows we want to protect her."

"Have you thought about *how* you're going to 'protect' her?"

"No, master. But we do intend to protect her and protect the capital at the same time."

Benar was touched to hear of this loyalty. "I hope you are able to carry out your intentions, Master Deben."

"Thank you for your help, Master Benar."

"Certainly, certainly. I only wish there were more I could do."

"Your work with the barren is very admirable, Master."

Benar only gave a slight nod in acknowledgment of this compliment, but she liked hearing it.

"Master Deben, there's something I've been wondering about."

"Yes, Master Benar?"

"The barren who attacked Master Udow—she was captured, wasn't she?"

"Yes, she was. We released her in the desert. There's been no sign of her since."

"Was she ever identified?"

"No."

"Do you think she might have been a server?"

"We have no way of knowing, Master. When we found her, she wasn't wearing any robe." For nearly a novade, the servers had withdrawn from capital life even more than was customary. Whatever servers who developed barren syndrome might exist, they did not access the help of the caretaker corps. Any treatment or restraining efforts apparently took place within the temple. The reluctance of the servers to communicate openly about the syndrome left the masters with serious doubts about how they were dealing with it.

Benar, with her middle-aged face, and Deben, younger, but wise with experience, shared eye contact and knew they were both thinking the same thing.

"What is going on in there?" asked Deben, almost whispering.

"I don't know," said Benar, "but there does seem to be something wrong, doesn't there?" There was nothing more that could be said. Deben thanked Benar and left.

Just then, a young caretaker master came around the corner with three little child-uedin. They were jumping and dancing around her. One of them was tugging playfully on the back of her belt.

"Master Bevol, make us some sweetpepper biscuits!"

"I'm going to make a great big sweetpepper biscuit and eat it all by myself!" teased the young master.

"Nooo!" they squealed and giggled. "Make a sweetpepper biscuit THIS BIG! Then we can all eat it!"

"Make a sweetpepper biscuit as big as a table!" they jumped up and down with delight. Benar looked on wistfully, recalling the days when she had served as a regular caretaker to the unnamed.

Part 4

PUREST EXERCISE

The Server Tilke

The lesser moon was full and the greater moon was new. On such days the servers of the central temple ate a meal of seeds. There were many bowls, each containing a different variety of edible seed. The bowls were circulated with great attention, and each server took some seeds from each bowl to eat in a slow and meditative exercise.

"*Hunnnnnnn …*" Chanting commenced throughout the meal. Each note was sustained for long periods. A small polished bowl was passed to Tilke. She watched a hand, her own, come up and receive the bowl as it was passed to her from a server seated beside her.

"*Nnnnnnn …*" the tone droned on. Beautiful blue and black pillflower seeds filled the bottom of a bowl that was in her hand. A favorite of the Soft One, Tilke knew without needing to be told. Fingers reached into a bowl held in a hand to take a seed.

"*Nnnnnnn …*" Tilke regarded with neutral awareness a sensation of her shoulder muscles functioning. Muscles at her upper arm constricted to draw a hand to a face. A seed came into a mouth.

"*Baaaaaa* ..." Ears received the sound of other servers' voices producing a next note. Lips had closed over a seed, so the initial sound of the *baa* did not sound in the mouth that took the seed, but ears comprehended that it had been initiated in unified voices all around. Lips parted to make the *aa* continuance.

"*Aaaaaaa* ..." The sound of the *aa* reverberated from the back of a mouth up and down a spine, filling the skull with the sound of the "aa" and producing a vibration into a chest. As a tongue gently directed a seed to back teeth, arm muscles contracted and drew. A polished bowl of pillflower seeds was directed to a server seated on the other side.

"*Aaaaaaaa* ..." Tilke knew, without needing to be told, how the Soft One took pleasure in the sensation of jaws coming together with force to crush the pillflower seed. To chew, the *aa* was suspended internally, but it continued outside. Top and bottom teeth clamped and drew against each other, the shell of the seed breaking up into woody bits. A flavor so delicious was the gift of the pillflower. The Soft One was very happy to be able to share its deliciousness.

"*Muuuuuuu* ..." The chewed seed was reduced between teeth to a small bit of gritty pulp. Its flavor was completely released. Gravity pulled on a body frame. Blood pumped through a body, delivering warmth to feet and hands. There was an amazement about the freedom of movement—even while the body sat still, the potentiality of its standing up or its walking away created a cloud of pregnant energy. Tilke felt gratitude and love pouring into her. This was the glory and awesome truth of serverhood. It was to share the experience of uedin life with the Soft One, and in turn to touch Her own dark and quiet existence.

"*Uuuuuuuu* …" A small white bowl with tiny black milk-grass seeds …

Later, Tilke drank tea and shared a game of hook blocks with one of the older servers. There were times when it was necessary to draw back into normal uedin experience and leave the Lern alone. She was interested in most of the labor and activity of the temple, but there were a few things She didn't like. Once Tilke was sharing her experience with Her when she discovered an infestation of mice in a storehouse. At the first thought of exterminating them she felt Her profound revulsion, even though it was something that had to be done for the good of the temple. Since then she had learned that there were many things that the Soft One didn't want to share in. She disliked any sort of contest. So when it became necessary to relax and have some recreation with the other servers, the Lern was left alone.

"Haha!" said the old server. Tilke didn't know her name. The servers rarely bothered with names. "There's a root hook at you! Now try to beat that one, young server!" The old ro-server's eye's sparkled with fun.

"Here." Tilke placed a circle block at one of her opponent's root hooks. It wasn't going to turn the game to her advantage yet, but it would slow things down.

"Oh! You're trying to stop me, aren't you?" shouted the ro-uedin with glee.

Before coming to the central temple, Tilke had mainly considered her own suitability for becoming a server and had not thought much about what the life of the community would be like. When she entered, she had not found it to be an easy adjustment. The mood was too somber, the sense of confinement too oppressive. From that uneasy beginning and through her gradual embracing of the server life, what stood out in her mind was the feeling that it had been a strange accident that had delivered her there. There was a puzzle in the events of having been led to the Soft One by a childhood friend who then declined to enter the temple with her. But gradually she stopped thinking about the events that had led her there. The Soft One drew her mind away from the question of *why* and *how*.

By listening, and by opening her heart and mind, she learned what She loved and what She recoiled from. Her love and appreciation of life and beauty was so deep! When she learned to share her eyes with the Soft One, the branch of an aged tree in the temple garden rising and falling gently with a breeze became beautiful and lovely in a way that she couldn't have imagined before. Such experiences convinced her that the Soft One was real. Servers believed that Lern Beyana actually had a physical body that rested somewhere in a stationary form. Certainly She was much too frail and withdrawing to reside anywhere near the capital. But Her location didn't matter. She loved the uedin, Tilke knew that. They were all like darling unnamed child-uedin to Her.

Tilke had learned by paying attention to the older servers that the Soft One seemed to conceal a secret hurt. Their comments and decisions implied that they understood Her to be shielding them from this hurt in the same way that they shielded Her from the necessary temple activities She disliked. The ro-servers acknowledged this to each other with the subtlest nods and glances, and Tilke came to understand that this secret hurt was something not to be probed. The time eventually came for Tilke to spend a whole season in the inner sanctuary. Every moment was shared with Lern Beyana there—even bathing and toileting were undertaken with ritualized humility and attentiveness to accommodate the Soft One's presence. But in that space, after a time, one truly began to forget one's uedin identity. And when the Lern's consciousness filled her, Tilke started to experience hints of Her secret sorrows and pains. These were not experiences to be sought out, but when they happened, the servers understood that the Soft One needed and loved them as much as they needed and loved Her.

"I've got you now!" shouted the old server and stomped her foot. She put a triple hook block down on the table.

"Yes, you have. You've beaten me," Tilke said with grin.

Assignment to Redrock Outvillage

A small community of uedin had lived in the outvillage of Redrock more than sixty generations. It was famous for its hot springs, referred to occasionally in some of the ancient verses, and was the birthplace of Regam, a famous mathematician. The drycreek that fed the uedin population there had once been of considerable size. There were empty dwellings recalling the days when nearly two hundred uedin, mostly tin miners, had occupied the outvillage. Now there were only twenty-six, including the mere three child-uedin who had arrived with the most recent novade rains.

The central gathering hall at Redrock was an old crumbling structure that recent surveys had deemed unsafe. The capital had provided plans and materials for restoration, but the outvillage lacked the hands to complete the job. Master Wanba, a senior guard at the Flatpools District station, had grown up at Redrock. She asked Elenn and Hela to go and help in the project.

It was a two-day trek from the capital under mid-summer sun. They wrapped themselves in light cloth and wore large shade hats. On the first day they reached the salt fields south of the western outfields. Elenn could have gone further, but she was self-conscious about her strength. She knew it was a development related to her barren syndrome. So when Hela asked if she wanted to keep on going a little further, Elenn said, "No, let's stop. I'm exhausted."

They had only minimal camping supplies. Each carried a thin sleeping mat rolled up together with a blanket, water gourds, and some dried food. Hela noticed that Elenn's behavior seemed nervous and anxious. The early evening sun was still bright, but Elenn started preparing a spot to sleep. She put down the woven mat, examined a corner that was coming apart, picked it up and fumbled to fix the weave with shaky fingers. She dropped the mat and looked at the small patch of ground she was going to sleep on. She decided she wanted to get rid of some bumps, so she started trying to remove rocks that were solidly buried in the hard white ground by scratching around them with her bare hands. Hela watched her with concern.

"Master Elenn, what are you doing? Do you need some help?"

Elenn, unaware that Hela had been watching her, looked up with some surprise. "Is there something else I need to do now?" asked Elenn timidly. She seemed to be afraid of making a mistake.

"No, I'm offering to help if you need it." Hela knew about Elenn's condition. All the guards knew now. It was a special kind of challenge to know how to balance respectful directness with sensitive accommodation.

"Thank you, Master Hela." Elenn sat down on the ground and looked at Hela with smiling eyes that sparkled through pain. "We are both from Quarterhouse, aren't we, Master Hela?"

"Yes we are. Same generation."

"We learned our codes and verses together, didn't we Master Hela?" Elenn was suddenly very emotional. "We took name together."

Hela decided to try to direct Elenn's attention to the landscape. "What do you think of these salt fields? They're beautiful, don't you think?" The early evening sun was just beginning to set. The beaming white salt flats were changing to a soft creamy yellow.

"Oh, yes, the salt fields are very beautiful," Elenn asserted immediately. Her tone implied that she was agreeing out of obedience rather than perception. "We should recite the Names now. Let's recite the Names."

Hela looked at Elenn with concern. This was not normal. Masters didn't just jump into Beyanic recitation in an instant.

"Lehera Beyana yana ya!" chanted Elenn in a mechanical-sounding voice. She looked over at Hela and gave her a nod. Hela looked back at her in disbelief.

Elenn said it again. "Lehera Beyana yana ya." She bent forward and whispered, "All right, now you repeat it. You repeat the name after me."

Elenn nodded, blinked and tried again. "Lehera Beya—"

"Master Elenn!" Hela shouted at her sternly.

Elenn looked back at her with surprise. "Oh, please forgive me Master Hela, you should initiate the recitation of Names, and I'll do the repetitions. Yes, of course, go ahead." She raised hands to face in humility.

"Master Elenn, please try to calm yourself," said Hela sternly. "You're in a very agitated state right now. This is not a good time to recite the Names of the Lern."

Elenn suddenly felt very ashamed of herself. She was acting like a barren. She must control herself! She must not allow herself to act like a barren!

Hela saw Elenn receive the admonishment with all its implications. Elenn's shoulders, which she now noticed to be appearing peculiarly large, slumped heavily around her bowing head as she gazed emptily at the ground.

"We'll be fine, Master Elenn. But let's try to have an easy time during this assignment. I'm very much looking forward to seeing the outvillage, aren't you?" Hela was trying to be kind.

Hela continued, "We don't have to worry about any schedules or our duties at the station. This will be a very nice time. We might even be able to enjoy the hot springs at Redrock."

Elenn's large hand gripped a corner edge of the large rock she had been picking at earlier. With a simple tug, she tore it up out of the solid salt and then threw it hard, out over the salt field. Her strength was more than a uedin should normally have, even a guard accustomed to hard physical labor. Hela was shocked. Was Elenn slipping into derangement? Did she have reason to be concerned for their safety?

When Elenn lifted her head, Hela could see that she had an angry expression, but there were tears in her eyes. She said in quiet but heavily punctuated speech, *"I—am—going—to—recite—the—Names."* She stood up and walked by herself to a spot twenty or thirty paces away, sat down on the white salt ground and faced the sun, which was now setting in golden hues.

"Lehera Beyana yana ya …"

She let silence fill in the space for the repetition which would normally be chanted.

"Lerna Beyana ulrana uedina …"

The setting sun, now reflecting a pink-orange glow down upon the salt fields, was as intense in its beauty as Elenn's heart was heavy with confusion and sadness.

"Lern Beyan kiman kiman uedin olorrr …"

Elenn heard footsteps behind her. *"Lern Beyan kiman kiman uedin olorrr …"* Hela chanted the echo with conviction.

"Hunna Bah muh Lor …"

"Hunna Bah muh Lor …" Hela positioned herself beside Elenn and continued chanting the echo with quiet understanding.

"Mei nar Lalem Lalem Paremm …"

"Mei nar Lalem Lalem Paremm …"

That night the two guards slept under a brilliant star-filled sky. Hela was refreshed by the clean air so far from the capital and fell asleep quickly, face down on her mat. Elenn spent much of the night in a sort of frozen position, gazing at the back of Hela's slender and healthy neck and head. The fat vein that ran up the back of Hela's skull pulsed softly. Elenn found herself transfixed with desire and shame. She wished that she could be an embryo, safely protected within the skullwomb of a healthy uedin, constantly nourished by the rich skullsap of her parent. It was a vain and misconceived thing to long for.

Arrival at Redrock

Elenn felt more focused and alert the next day. Hela dismissed her apologies with a generous wave of her hand. After another full day of walking, the two guards reached the outvillage of Redrock. It featured four clay-construction longhouses built at the foot of a bluff. The reconstruction of the gathering hall was already partly underway. Wooden reinforcements, which appeared to have been treated with some sort of mineral wash, stretched in web-like rows across the front face of the building.

There had been a time when travelers to the outvillage had been numerous, but in recent generations it was rare for any, other than the regular distributor masters, to visit Redrock. The residents were very excited to greet their guests. After a sleepless night and a long day of walking, Elenn was numb and exhausted, but she felt a definite thrill when they walked into the center of the outvillage and everyone came out to meet them. The clothing of the Redrock outvillagers was dyed in unusual colors derived from algae and silts found at the nearby mineral hot springs and boiling mud pools.

"Welcome! How good that you've come!" The outvillagers beamed with enthusiasm. Elenn and Hela smiled and repeatedly drew their hands over their mouths in gratitude.

PUREST EXERCISE

A short and corpulent ro-uedin introduced herself. "We're very happy to have you as our guests. My name is Urpa. This is Master Gefla, and Master Betol is over there." She pointed to some of the other ro-uedin. They raised hands to face in greeting. "Master Gefla has made a nice supper of boiled grain! And we have fresh pickles and yeastdrink! But first we'll let you rest in the long house and have a bath before supper. Come along!"

Elenn noticed the three child-uedin skipping together with excitement among the small crowd. They were, of course, the same age as the unnamed back at the capital, but it seemed odd to find such little ones living out here.

After the guests from the capital were shown their spaces with fresh sleeping mats in the longhouse, they were invited to leave their bundles there and follow Urpa and Gefla past a few seemingly abandoned small buildings. The decline in population was evidenced by the presence of facilities long unused. When they came around a small grove of bubbleleaf trees they saw the steam of the mineral springs. The bathing pools, cut right out of the rock in the early days of the outvillage, were worn smooth with age and regular use. There were two other uedin there. One was using a bucket and cloth to wash herself after a day of work in the mine. The other sat immersed in the hot water, enjoying a soak.

"We hope you enjoy our mineral springs," said Gefla.

"I'm certain we will, thank you very much master," said Hela with a smile.

"You'll have plenty of time to bathe and have a rest in the longhouse. Someone will come for you when it's time for supper. While the gathering hall is under repair, we've been having our suppers in the grand mine. Oh, and there are towels and buckets in the hut over there. Can you find your way back to the longhouse?"

"Yes. Thank you Master Gefla," said Elenn.

"Isn't this a wonderful assignment!" said Hela to Elenn as the outvillage master disappeared around the bubbleleaf trees.

"It's good to be given such a welcome," said Elenn.

After obtaining buckets and towels from the hut, Elenn and Hela washed quickly and then stepped gingerly down into the steaming pools. The water was hotter than what they were used to at Flatpools.

The old ro-uedin soaking at the end of the pool laughed. "Don't hedge so much—it just makes it harder to adjust to the hot water. You will do better if you just come right in!"

Elenn and Hela looked at each other and shared a smile, acknowledging their common cowardice. Elenn was glad that they were able to put the awkwardness of the previous night behind them. It was because of Hela's kindness and her willingness to act as though nothing troublesome had occurred. She was so grateful to Hela.

"Maybe by the time we're finished with our work here, we'll get used to these hot springs enough to jump right in," said Hela with a smile.

They gradually adjusted and positioned themselves. Elenn found that if she kept her hands and feet still, the hot water was more tolerable. The initial sting slowly gave way to deep relaxation. The heat of the mineral water permeated their muscles and bones.

"This is much hotter than the baths at the capital," commented Elenn.

The ro-uedin at the other end of the pool opened her eyes and nodded. "Yes, I was in the capital once for some medical training. I couldn't believe how lukewarm the baths were. Not at all hot enough down there, oh no …" she muttered, and closed her eyes again.

After a few minutes, Hela closed her own eyes and let her head lean backwards, her skullwomb resting against the ledge. Elenn watched her for a moment and noticed how her skullsap vein curled when she leaned her head backwards. She didn't want to look at it any more, so she repositioned herself to face another way and closed her eyes to concentrate on the calming hot soak.

This assignment had been arranged for her intentionally, Elenn knew. Master Wanba and Master Deben knew that she was showing symptoms of her barren syndrome. Did they think the excursion would be good for her? The Redrock mineral springs were supposed to have medicinal benefits. But even if they had only sent her because they felt sorry for her and wanted her to have a pleasant experience, it didn't matter. Elenn was no longer proud or defensive when it came to her fellow guards' sympathy. She only appreciated it and wanted not to take it for granted. She thought of the previous day's sunset over the salt flats. Despite the unpleasant feelings she had about how she had acted there, the amazing beauty of it had made enough of an impression to linger with her. And now she was here in this extraordinary place, being treated as a guest in a manner she had never experienced before. Perhaps she could forget her troubles for a while and try to enjoy the wonderful things around her. She took a deep breath, inhaling the vapors.

After a long and pleasant soak in the mineral baths and a short rest in the longhouse, Elenn and Hela were met by Urpa, the outvillage ro who had greeted them earlier. She led them past the longhouses all the way to the rocky wall of the bluff, at which point they turned and followed a path that went along the wall.

"Since our gathering hall is under repair, we have been using the grand mine as our gathering space," said Urpa. "It's a bit dark—hope you don't mind."

Hela and Elenn followed Urpa into a framed opening in the rock wall and found themselves in near total darkness. There were a few pathetically weak lamps burning here and there, a couple attached to the inside wall of the cavernous space, a few others placed on what appeared to be a table. The light provided was only enough to illuminate tiny areas immediately around the lamps. Elenn could not see her feet, and could barely see her own hand when she held it in front of her face. How could they possibly do anything in such a dark space?

"Master Urpa, forgive me, but I can't see a thing," said Hela.

"Oh that's fine, it will only take a few minutes for your eyes to adjust. You can put your hand on my shoulder if you like," responded Urpa. Elenn decided she needed to join this caravan, put her hand up, and found what she hoped was Hela's shoulder.

"Is that you Master Hela?" whispered Elenn.

"Yes."

"Have you got Master Urpa's shoulder?"

"Yes."

"Are your eyes adjusting?"

"Well … no," whispered Hela.

"Neither are mine."

Elenn heard light footsteps and giggling as the child-uedin rushed around their legs and in ahead of them.

"Master Urpa, it's amazing how your community has developed an ability to adjust to such dark spaces."

"Well, we've always been miners here," Urpa said jovially. They heard the sound of a bench being drawn out. Feeling the bench bump her legs, Elenn climbed over it one foot at a time and sat down. She was pretty sure that she was sitting beside Hela.

"Can't you see yet?" asked Urpa.

"No, master."

"Master Reta!" she called, "Our guests need a little more light. Will you light more lamps?"

"Certainly," said a voice. Elenn saw just a hint of a uedin's face leaning over one of the dim lamps. A little stick was used to catch the flame of the burning lamp and light two others that were then placed on the tabletop close to where Elenn and Hela were seated. It did not improve visibility at all.

Urpa commenced to introduce others to them one after another. She was oblivious to the fact that they couldn't see the uedin to whom they were being introduced.

"... and this is Master Ib'ow."

"Welcome to Redrock," said a voice.

"Thank you Master Ib'ow." Elenn and Hela spoke the same words simultaneously. They didn't know which of them was meeting Master Ib'ow first. Elenn made the greeting gesture in the dark to whoever Master Ib'ow was, hoping she was facing in the right direction.

There was incredible racket echoing all around them as the outvillagers laughed and talked loudly as if they were at a perfectly normal banquet. They could be heard talking with their mouths full as they gobbled and gabbed at the same time. A huge bowl was slammed down in front of Elenn, and then she heard the sound of heaps of boiled grain being ladled into the bowl. She reached forward, found a large metal spoon, and grasped the wooden bowl. She picked it up to see how full it was. There was at least four or five times as much in it as she was used to getting back at the station in the capital. She tasted it and found it to be deliciously spiced, but she thought the portion was ridiculously large and didn't know how she was going to eat it all. Then she heard a child-uedin giggling uncontrollably, and a little voice said, "The capital master is eating from one of the serving dishes!" Everyone around them erupted into loud guffaws. Elenn was momentarily embarrassed, but being in the dark somehow made her feel less self-conscious. She joined in the laughter. She found the smaller bowl and held it while someone filled it with a reasonable portion.

"Have as much as you like, Master Elenn." It was Master Urpa who was filling her bowl. "We know you must be hungry after two days of travel. Have some of these pickles too. There are two kinds—ballroot and yellowstem." Some pickles were tossed into Elenn's bowl right on top of the boiled grain.

"Little one," Urpa addressed one of the unnamed, "bring some yeastdrink for the capital masters."

"I'll help!" said a small voice.

"Me too!" another.

The scurry of small child-uedin feet rushed off. Elenn was amazed that they were apparently able to see where they were going. In a few moments she could hear the little huffing and puffing of child-uedin carrying the heavy filled cups and using all their might to place them them cautiously on the table top. After three or four good swallows of yeastdrink, both Elenn and Hela relaxed about being in the dark. It was a welcoming party for them, the outvillagers seemed genuinely delighted to have them, and there was nothing to do but eat, drink, and enjoy themselves.

The night turned into a swirl of noise, laughter, child-ue-dins' recited verses, cups and cups of yeastdrink, and detailed explanations about pickling and tin mining. All of this took place in the dark of the mine. Elenn and Hela did find that their eyes adjusted to the darkness ever so slightly, just enough to see a face here, a cup there. There was no mention of the repair work on the gathering hall until the next morning.

Hearing and Telling of Stories

The brilliant sunlight streaming in the windows of the longhouse made a dramatic contrast to the dark of the previous night's festivities. Elenn was fascinated by the decor of the longhouse. On the outside it appeared as a simple blockish structure. Its interior, on the other hand, was beautifully adorned with intricately shaped pieces of tin plating that caught the sunlight from the windows and filled the space with darts of light.

After a breakfast of tea and more pickles, Elenn and Hela were shown the plans for repairing the gathering hall that had been provided by building masters in the capital. They mainly called for wooden reinforcements of the exterior walls. Since there was little timber anywhere near the outvillage, a generous amount had been transported all the way from the capital. The wood was handled with great respect. What Elenn had perceived to be some sort of stain turned out to be coloration caused by the soaking of the wood in mineral springs. The outvillagers said that the mineral soak reduced the likelihood of dry rot. A third of the wood had already been used; the remainder lay in neat stacks beside the gathering hall.

Four of the outvillage masters had been assigned to construction work while the rest of the community carried on their normal mining and service assignments. Elenn and Hela were somewhat relieved to learn that the outvillagers understood the plans well and would not be relying on them to help solve any engineering problems. Though the population of the outvillage continued to dwindle, they clung to a commitment to maintain their usual operations as a way of asserting their determination to stay in the outvillage and work there as long as Great Rains would continue to send them wetuedin at the beginning of each novade. They were grateful to have assistance with labor on the reconstruction project from Elenn and Hela so that they could continue in their regular work.

Elenn and Hela worked all day with the four outvillagers. They were all physically strong and enduring as a result of their regular mining work. It made sense that guards, who likewise engaged in more physical work than most uedin in the capital, had been recruited for assistance. Elenn was particularly effective. She was self-conscious about her size and strength. Only Hela might make the connection with barren syndrome, she thought, but she was nevertheless slightly ashamed of this advantage.

At midday, Master Urpa came with tea and fieldpears. As they lunched, she talked about the child-uedin.

"When I was unnamed there was a school. We had seventeen in my generation here. They all took assignments in the capital after receiving name, except for me and Master Rula.

Every novade seems to bring fewer wetuedin, and few remain after taking name. As you know we only have three unnamed right now." she sighed. "I suppose this is how a lot of outvillages faded away."

"Why do you think your drystream delivers fewer than before?" asked Hela.

"The novade rains just run to the other streams." said Urpa. "It's probably the natural course of things. Streams do change their courses, you know."

"Yes," said Elenn, "some of the drystreams close to the capital have seriously shifted. The guards had to do quite a bit of reinforcement at the last novade's rains to keep the streams intact."

"The capital pools are receiving the usual numbers of wetuedin, I assume?" asked Urpa.

"I believe there were about three hundred and sixty total that came with the last Great Rains," said Hela.

Urpa looked puzzled. The number was low. She expected the numbers to be higher since wetuedin were not coming to Redrock. If they weren't coming to the outvillage, and they weren't going to the capital, where were they going?

"Only three hundred and sixty?" she finally said.

"I'm not sure exactly, but I think there are about three hundred and sixty of the new generation in the capital," said Hela, trying to sound casual. She noticed Urpa's perplexed regard. She knew that the explanation was bound to the increasing occurrence of barren syndrome, but she was reluctant to mention the subject in Elenn's presence.

"Such a low number …" said Urpa.

Elenn looked away, focusing her vision on nothing in particular, and spoke rather quietly, "You must know, Master Urpa, that barren syndrome has been on the increase in the capital."

"Ah … Shield the Lern …" said Urpa with realization. "Yes, the barren."

"We are struggling to cope with the syndrome in the capital," said Hela, nibbling the core of a fieldpear and trying not to be too emphatic. "It is affecting us all."

While Urpa paused before responding, Elenn wondered how far the discussion would go. She knew that her fellow guard would not tell the outvillagers about her own being barren, but the degree to which the barren had disrupted uedin life in the capital was hardly something that would ordinarily be left undiscussed. Udow's death alone had shaken the capital. On some level she felt that the situation should be shared with Redrock, but Hela was being considerate of her, and she felt unprepared to talk about it herself. She said nothing.

Finally Urpa spoke. "I knew there was an increase in barren, but I didn't imagine it was causing smaller generations. What a horrible thing." Again there was an uncomfortable pause. Then Urpa added, "I remember once a barren appeared here at Redrock."

"Tell us about it, Master Urpa," Elenn said, trying not to appear too interested. "Was it a long time ago?"

"Oh yes. At that time there was no knowledge here that barren even existed. I remember it well. I must have been only second or third generation at the time. Some of our miners had found a uedin huddling in one of the mines. She was naked, filthy, and her skin was very raw. They brought her into the village and tried to help her. She would not speak except to say over and over that she was hungry. She didn't appear to be starving, but she kept saying how hungry she was."

Hela was uncomfortable hearing about this with Elenn listening, but she didn't know what to say.

Elenn remained very calm. "What happened to her?"

"They tried to give her food, but she refused it even while groaning about how hungry she was. She stayed in the community for a few days, and then one morning she became violent and attacked one of our ro-uedin."

"She attacked a ro-uedin?" asked Elenn, feeling more sad than horrified.

"Yes, the ro nearly died. At that point they decided that it was going to be necessary to take the stranger to the capital. Some thought she had been poisoned and were hoping that the medic masters at the capital would be able to help. A few miners were taken off the job to escort her on the journey. I believe they had to sedate her so that she would cooperate enough to let them lead her away. It didn't work out though. Before they reached the capital, the stranger somehow managed to escape and run away."

"And while all this happened you didn't even know you were dealing with a barren?"

"No one here at Redrock had heard of the barren," said Urpa, "We only thought it was a stranger who had something terribly wrong with her. We never even learned her name. Later we had other visitors from the capital who heard the story and told us we had been hosting a barren."

"You never determined what happened to her afterwards?" asked Hela.

"No," Urpa spoke with her mouth full of fieldpear, "we never saw or heard of her again." She smiled oddly, dismissing the topic with a shrug and took a big swallow of tea. They all finished their meal and went back to work.

That evening after another meal shared in the darkness but without the yeastdrink and much less commotion, the three child-uedin gathered around Elenn and Hela asking questions about the capital.

"Is it true the streets in the capital are covered with little square rocks fitted together?" These child-uedin were far more informal in their speech and manner toward adult uedin than unnamed in the capital. Elenn and Hela were fascinated by their boldness.

"Yes, it's true. We had to repair some areas after the last Great Rains—the same Rains that delivered you to Redrock." said Hela.

"Do you have mineral springs in the capital?"

"No, we have some very large baths there, but no mineral springs. We like your mineral springs very much."

"Have you seen the boiling muds yet?" asked another of the child-uedin.

"No, we haven't," said Hela. "Could you show them to us some time?"

"Master Urpa, can we take Master Elenn and Master Hela to the boiling muds tonight?" asked the unnamed.

"Oh, not tonight, little one, it's much too late. If you finish your lessons early one day before they leave, maybe Master Elenn and Master Hela will go with you to see our boiling muds." The three child-uedin clapped with excitement.

"Can you tell us a story from the capital?" asked one of them.

"Yes! Tell us a capital story!" the other two chimed in.

Elenn and Hela did not know how to respond. They were unaccustomed to such requests.

"That might be nicely entertaining," said one of the other outvillage masters. "We might all enjoy a story from one of the capital masters."

"Would either of you be willing to indulge us?" asked Urpa.

"I'm afraid I am quite inept at such things," said Hela, "but perhaps Master Elenn could tell you one."

Elenn looked at her colleague. "Master Hela, surely you could give a good telling …"

"I knew from early on I was going to be a guardmaster," said Hela. "I paid little attention to the stories and codes at Quarterhouse."

"Yes, tell us a story from Quarterhouse!" said one of the child-uedin. They had heard of Quarterhouse, where unnamed child-uedin like themselves took their training by the hundreds.

"Well I'm not quite sure what story would be good …" Elenn remembered many of the stories from the oral tradition of Quarterhouse. Many were jumbled myths with circuitous plots or stories about earlier generations of Quarterhouse masters and unnamed that held little interest for outsiders.

"How about the story of the vadime and the hailflower?" suggested Hela.

"Oh we have a little song about the hailflower, but no story here at Redrock," said Urpa. "We would enjoy hearing that."

"What's a vadime, Master Urpa?" asked one of the unnamed.

"A vadime? A vadime is a mythical air-spirit. It can turn into many things."

"The vadime story is rather sad, don't you think, Master Hela?" said Elenn with concern.

"But the unnamed will be able to follow it," said Hela.

"Very well." said Elenn, and she began to introduce the story. "The story of vadime and the hailflower tells of a time very long ago, before there was even a capital, and before there were any uedin."

"Before there were uedin?" asked one of the child-uedin in astonishment. "Even before Lern Beyana?"

"Lern Beyana?" repeated Elenn thoughtfully, realizing that the vadime story must predate Beyanic time. "As a matter of fact, yes—it was a time even before there was a Lern Beyana." Elenn noted that her audience accepted this with unexpected ease.

"Wait, let me get everyone's attention …" said Urpa. "Masters! Masters!" She waited for the conversations all around to cease. Elenn was somewhat relieved by the fact that she couldn't see her listeners, even if they were quite used to the dark and able to see her well enough. "Our guest, Master Elenn, has agreed to give us a recitation of a story from Quarterhouse in the capital!" The room was quiet. "Little ones, once Master Elenn begins her story, you must not ask her any questions until the end. She's reciting from the Quarterhouse oral tradition, so we mustn't interrupt her. Please commence, Master Elenn."

"I have not done recitation since before I took name," said Elenn, "So please be patient if I stumble. This will be the story of the vadime and the hailflower tree." And so Elenn began with the regulated voice of recitation that she had learned from the Quarterhouse masters.

"You have all seen, at some time or other, the beautiful hailflower tree, known to us all as the loveliest tree of the forest. Have you wondered why it is that while the hailflower boasts sweet flowers, minty roots, and beautiful dark green leaves, it never produces any fruit? It is because of what happened very long ago when vadime lived in the land and gave birth to all the living things of the forest."

Elenn's oratory voice carried very well in the dark. Everyone present including the child-uedin were completely still, so much so that in the darkness she felt as if she were telling the story to no one but herself.

"Once there was a gentle-mannered and lovely vadime who gave birth to a hailflower tree. It was a very beautiful tree and grew quite fast. When it was one year old, it put forth lovely flowers on its branches. The vadime, meanwhile, came under

some sort of a strange illness that caused her to feel terribly hungry, and yet no matter what she ate, the hunger refused to subside. When the vadime smelled the sweet and spicy scent of the hailflowers, she knew in her heart that only by eating the flowers would she have any relief from the terrible hunger. The hailflower tree sensed its mother's sadness and asked, 'What is wrong, my dear Mother-vadime? Are the flowers not lovely that blossom on my boughs?'

"The vadime replied, 'Your boughs in bloom are a joy to my eyes, but a knife to my heart, for I have a strange illness that causes me to hunger and yet nothing I eat will banish it. Now I have smelled the sweet perfume of your flowers and know that if I do not eat the flowers I will die. But in my mother-vadime's heart I cannot think of touching your lovely flowers.'

"The hailflower tree was shocked by the words of its mother-vadime. But then it said, 'I also cannot bear to have my mother-vadime come upon me to feed so, but listen. Every day a wild goat comes rummaging and eating the weeds under my branches and knocks carelessly about. I do not care for the goat, but neither do I mind that goat. If you take the form of that wild goat, then I will not know it is you who comes, and when you eat my flowers I will not know it is you.'

"'Truly you are the dearest one to me in all the world,' said the vadime, and went away in tears.

"The following morning, the mother-vadime came back and found the hailflower tree had suffered the loss of all its lovely sweet flowers.

"'Poor child!' cried the vadime, 'What has happened to you?'

"'Oh, never mind, Mother-vadime,' said the hailflower tree, 'It was just that awful old goat. She came in the night and ate all of my flowers. Perhaps next spring I will be taller, and she won't be able to reach. For now, there's nothing I can do about it, so let us never mind.'

"'Truly you are the dearest one to me in all the world,' said the vadime, and went away in tears.

"The next day the mother-vadime came back. The vadime was very deeply pained in her heart because the hunger was not gone. The vadime caught sight of a bit of the hailflower tree's root that grew around a rock and into the ground. The root emitted a sweet pungent smell that the vadime was unbearably drawn to.

"The vadime realized with a horrible sorrow that her disease of hunger was consuming her once again. She tried to sate herself with river plants and wild bulbs, yet no matter what she ate, the hunger refused to subside. The vadime knew in her heart that only by eating the fleshy roots of the hailflower would she have any relief from the terrible hunger. The hailflower tree sensed its mother's sadness and asked, 'What is wrong, my dear Mother-vadime? Is not the scent of my spicy roots pleasing to you?'

"The vadime replied, 'The perfume of your sweet roots is as lovely as the spring flowers, but a knife to my heart, for I have a strange illness that causes me to hunger and yet nothing I eat will banish it. Now I have smelled the spice of your roots and know that if I do not eat of them I will die. But in my mother-vadime's heart I cannot bear to touch you.'

"The hailflower tree was again shocked and saddened by the words of its mother-vadime. But then it said, 'I also cannot bear to have my mother-vadime come upon me to feed so. But listen. The wild goat who so treacherously ate up my flowers still comes to graze the weeds under my branches and knocks carelessly about. I do not care for the goat, but neither do I mind that goat. If you take the form of that wild goat, then I will not know it is you who comes, and when you eat of my roots, I will not know it is you.'

"'Truly you are the dearest one to me in all the world,' said the vadime, and went away in tears.

"The following morning the mother-vadime came back and found the hailflower tree had been nearly unearthed by some intruder who had ravaged its roots in the night.

"'Poor child!' cried the vadime, 'What has happened to you?'

"'Oh, never mind, Mother-vadime,' said the hailflower tree, 'It was just that awful old goat. She came in the night and tore and ate at my roots. Perhaps next spring my roots will have grown deeper, and she won't be able to reach. For now, there's nothing I can do about it, so let us never mind.'

"'Truly you are the dearest one to me in all the world,' said the vadime, and went away in tears.

"The next day the mother-vadime came back. The vadime was very deeply pained in her heart because the hunger was still not gone. As the vadime approached the hailflower tree, the first thing that came into her view was the succulent thickness of the hailflower's shiny green leaves. The leaves were fat with juice, and here and there, where there were little cuts and tears from the previous days' ravaging, drops of milk clung to the leaf tips and stems. The vadime found herself unbearably drawn to these dark, fleshy leaves.

"The vadime was so horrified to think that she would so hunger for her daughter's leaves, that she turned and ran away. She hid in the river for many hours, until she heard her daughter the hailflower tree calling out in a lonely voice.

"'Oh, Mother-vadime, you always come to visit me every morning. Have you spurned me because I no longer have my sweet flowers and pungent roots? Are not my leaves a pretty enough sight to make you remember your love for me?'

"The vadime could feel her heart breaking inside of her, and could not refrain from answering back, 'The green, green leaves that adorn your branches are a blessing to my eyes, but a knife to my heart, for my wretched illness causes me to hunger without relief. Now I have seen the lusciousness of your leaves and know that if I do not eat of them I will die. But in my mother-vadime's heart I cannot bear to touch you and would be therefore so much happier to die.'

"The hailflower tree was again filled with sadness by the words of its mother-vadime. But then it said, 'I also cannot bear to have my mother-vadime come upon me to feed so. But listen. The wild goat who gobbled my flowers and roots still comes to graze the weeds under my branches and is sure to come again. The goat preys upon me but causes me no great grief, since I care not about that goat. If you take the form of that wild goat, then

I will not know it is you who comes, and when you eat my leaves I will not know it is you. Only one thing do I ask: let one leaf remain on my branch, so that I can live to bear new flowers and leaves, to grow new roots next spring, and perhaps even to bear fruit when summer's end comes again.'

"'Truly you are the dearest one to me in all the world,' said the vadime, and went away in tears.

"The following morning, the mother-vadime came back and found the hailflower tree was bare. It was so weak and damaged, having lost all its flowers, roots and leaves, that it did not speak or stir. It stood in brittle stillness as if winter had come early.

"'Poor child! What has happened to you?' cried the mother-vadime. But the hailflower tree did not respond. It was nearly dead. It lingered in a sleepy state, its last spark of attention apparently focused on a single leaf, which quivered at the tip of its highest branch where the goat had not been able to reach.

"The vadime thought for a moment, and then with tears in her eyes, she rolled on the ground and turned into a goat —then she quietly walked to the hailflower tree, stretched her head up and plucked the last leaf with her goat-mouth. The hailflower tree trembled slightly and then let go its last flicker of life.

"Just as the vadime resumed her vadime form, there was a rustling in the bushes, and a real wild goat came stumbling into the spot where she was weeping by the dead hailflower tree. The goat was round and fat. The fur around its mouth was white with the sap of the hailflower. Its face was sullied with dirt from chewing at roots.

"'Oh, I see you have had a leaf from the hailflower. Is it not a delicious meal?' asked the fat goat, wobbly with overeating.

"'The taste of the leaf is more delicious than anything I have ever eaten, yet it sticks in my throat and cuts my heart,' answered the vadime. 'For I promised to let one leaf remain, and I could not do it.'

"'Is it because you were too hungry to resist?' asked the goat, smiling her goatish smile.

"'No,' said the vadime, 'Indeed I have starved all this time. Hunger I could resist, but my daughter's suffering I could not bear. I knew from the beginning that my daughter the hailflower was much too wise to believe her own stories about you, wild goat, eating her flowers and roots and leaves. I knew in my mother-vadime's heart that after she had told me to take your form before eating from her, she could never imagine that it was you indeed coming to ravage her in the night. For you see, a vadime can see into her daughter's heart. A vadime can see when her daughter sacrifices all, and feigns not knowing. Oh if she could have known that I starved but never touched her. Her suffering was greatest when she secretly thought her mother was destroying her but uttered not a word of this pain to spare her mother-vadime any sorrow. A vadime can see when her daughter suffers so terribly but pretends not to suffer. I knew what was happening, how her heart was breaking, but what could I say? Only could I weep in sorrow, and my sorrow broke always into aching hunger again. Until finally I saw in her dark and tortured heart the only bit of hope she had left. She began to hope her lies were true. She began to think *that maybe the wild goat really was the one destroying her, and that her dear mother-vadime had done nothing of the kind. She fought with herself, trying to believe this. It was her only prayer for peace. A vadime can see when her daughter thinks these things. She did not know I could see into her heart, but I could. At the end, my daughter said to herself that she would know the truth and die in peace. When the wild goat ate her last leaf, she would know it was she—not her mother-vadime—who had ravaged her all along. Then she could rest in the love of her mother vadime even as she let go of life. But if one leaf were spared, even though this might allow her to live, it would mean that her mother-vadime had done all this cruelty to her, and then she would live always with the sorrow of having been brutally treated by her mother-vadime. I reconciled myself to her death and watched you, wild goat, as you came and ate all the beautiful leaves from my daughter's branches. But when your belly was full, and when you were too lazy to stretch your neck, what did you do? You left one leaf untouched, didn't you, wild goat? And finally I knew the terrible thing I had to do for my dear daughter. I knew that rather than let her live to suffer, thinking that her mother-vadime had destroyed her, I had to let her die with the thought that it was that old goat who had killed her. So I changed into your form, wild goat, and I took her last leaf. And when her last leaf was plucked, I saw how my daughter the hailflower tree felt a deep relief, realizing that her mother-vadime would never break her promise, and that it must have been the goat all along, not her loving mother. I saw her let go of her fears and die peacefully.'*

"As the goat ambled away carelessly, the vadime wept, and began to grow weary. From having eaten the single leaf of the hailflower, she felt a peaceful rest come over her. She slept for many days, and was never hungry again.

"This is the story of the vadime and the hailflower tree. From this story we know why it is that the beautiful hailflower tree, though it be the loveliest tree of the forest, bears no fruit, but boasts only its spicy-sweet flowers, thick, minty roots, and lustrous green leaves that when eaten bring about a deep and blissful sleep."

After a long pause of appreciation, the Redrock masters all tapped their cups on the table top and called out, "Well told! Well told, Master Elenn!"

The child-uedin patted her on the shoulders and thanked her for the story. They soon after cleared the tables and left the dark chamber. The stars were out in great brilliance as Elenn followed Hela and Urpa to the longhouse. Before and behind her, small groups of uedin quietly chatted on the road, but Elenn was silent. She had been hypnotized by her own telling of the vadime story. It had come back with startling clarity, and recalling it in adult life brought it to a whole new level of significance. She was dumbstruck by the queer truth of the vadime story.

Calamity Upon Calamity

Elenn and Hela worked with the masters assigned to the construction project for the next ten days without any troubles. It was straightforward and uncomplicated work. Everyday the outvillagers greeted them with friendly salutations. Elenn enjoyed spending the long days working in the open air and became fairly well acquainted with the outvillage masters who had been assigned to work along with them. Her worries, however, were not easily left behind. One of the outvillage masters, Master Nehu, was one generation her elder, the same as Master Deben. Nehu had a brightness and an energy in her eyes, but Elenn tried never to look at her. The first time she had met Nehu, Elenn had noticed the fat, pronounced vein that ran in a curve up the back of Nehu's neck to her skullwomb. Now, she felt ashamed of herself every time she saw her, regardless of the angle.

One afternoon as they were working, Elenn accidentally caught a glimpse of the vein on the back of Nehu's neck throbbing as Nehu took a break after hoisting some crossbeams to their position in the reinforcement wall. That night, when Elenn lay down and put her face against the flooring of the longhouse to sleep, a picture of Nehu floated into her mind.

Her beautiful neck stretched and strained as she worked in the sunlight. Then Elenn pictured Nehu tripping over some scrap lumber, getting a bad scrape on the back of her neck. Elenn hurried to help her and saw that the deep scratch had left some small exposed ruptures in the vein. Elenn looked at Nehu's disoriented expression and the drops of honey-colored skullsap beading up on the scrape. Elenn could not resist. Holding Nehu's shoulders, she opened her mouth and ran her tongue along the wound. Lying in the shadows of the longhouse, Elenn was horrified by the imaginings of her own mind, but at the thought of slowly licking the wet beads of skullsap from the neck of this outvillager, a well of excitement flowed through her, at once jarring and completely intoxicating. Immediately following was an ache that came over her from head to toe as she sank into shame and hopelessness.

The next morning, Nehu greeted Elenn with her usual boisterous cheer. Elenn did her best to appear friendly. The labor was slow and monotonous that day. The sky happened to be gray and overcast. They chopped straw into small bits, mixed it with clay and powderwax, and carefully packed it into the spaces between the imported wood boards.

At mid afternoon Elenn began to experience dizziness and her vision became slightly blurred. In her head she kept hearing a childhood rhyme repeated over and over. It was a line from an old verse that was sung as part of a common game they played in early unnamed times at Quarterhouse. It went: *The crow is busy dancing, doesn't eat our grain; While we laugh, the crop is ruined in the rain.* This was the rhyme sung when very small unnamed—smaller even than child-uedin Elenn had become acquainted with in the outvillage—played a simple game of jumping in and out of circles drawn in the dirt with a pointed stick. It had nothing to do with anything, but Elenn could not rid it from her mind. *The crow is busy dancing, doesn't eat our grain; While we laugh, the crop is ruined in the rain. The crow is busy dancing, doesn't eat our grain; While we laugh …* Elenn stood and looked up in the sky. Was it going to rain?

"Master Elenn you sure are looking brawny! We could use you in the mines if you'd care to stay with us!" Elenn's head turned to face the source of the voice. It was Master Nehu. Elenn peered at her quizzically. Nehu was wearing a jocular smile. She did not mean this invitation seriously, she was only jesting with Elenn. Elenn cocked her head. What if Nehu had said instead, "Master Elenn you are growing large even though you are past your time of growing. You are barren, and we all know it." Nehu's face blurred slightly in Elenn's vision and it looked as though her eyes were melting into tears. *The crow is busy dancing, doesn't eat our grain; While we laugh, the crop is ruined in the rain.*

"Is everything all right, Master Elenn?" asked Nehu. Elenn imagined her reaching behind her head with the straw-cutting tool. She felt dizzy, and the overcast sky looked like a ceiling that was being lowered closer and closer over their heads. She suddenly imagined Nehu cutting her skullsap vein with the straw-cutting tool, drawing a cupped hand across the back of her neck, and now licking her own skullsap from her fingers. Elenn squeezed her eyes shut to rid her mind of the image. What was the significance of the rhyme that kept playing on and on? *The crow is busy dancing, doesn't eat our grain; While we laugh, the crop is ruined in the rain.*

"We must not do that …" said Elenn quietly, feeling the back of her own neck and finding her own skullsap vein protruding far more than she had imagined. "We mustn't."

"Master Hela!" Nehu was calling for Elenn's colleague. Fear of embarrassment drew Elenn back to her senses.

Hela came around the corner of the gathering hall. "Did you call me, Master Nehu?"

"Something's wrong with Master Elenn. I think she might have stepped on a poison thistle or something. She's acting very strangely."

Elenn, regaining her senses, tried to dismiss their concern. "Please forgive me, I'm just a little tired. I'm fine really. I think I just need a drink of water."

Hela's face showed a look of painful recognition. She whispered to her, "Are you sure you're all right, Master Elenn?" Her tone and the look in her eyes conveyed the message: *I will help you conceal your condition, but you need to trust me and play along here.* Elenn looked at Hela with appreciation. Keeping her eyes fixed on Hela's, she said, "Perhaps I did step on a poison thistle." *You are my friend Master Hela—please help me get though this!* she thought. By now the other outvillage masters had stopped working and were listening to them.

"Let's get her some water. She needs to keep moving around until she recovers."

"Here's water!" said one of the other outvillage masters and rushed over to them with a gourd bottle.

"She should walk. I'll walk her to the longhouse," said Nehu.

"No," said Hela, "let me walk with her. We'll be fine. We're guards and we're perfectly used to these situations." Nehu looked reluctant to let Hela take charge of Elenn.

"You are our guests here—let me take Master Elenn to the longhouse."

"It's all right, really, Master Nehu. We have poison thistles near the capital as well," said Hela. Elenn was filled with gratitude to hear her companion tell a lie for her.

"I think I would be most comfortable walking with my fellow guard …" said Elenn. Her wits were returning now, but it was still necessary to complete the deception.

"Very well," Nehu addressed Hela. "After you've walked a little, go back to the longhouse and let Master Elenn sleep."

They started walking slowly. Elenn even limped slightly to complete the picture. They didn't turn around, but they could tell that the outvillage masters were watching them for a short while. Then they heard the sound of cutting tools and mixing again.

"Are you really all right now?" asked Hela.

"Yes, I think I'm going to be fine."

"Perhaps it would be best if we left for the capital tomorrow morning, Master Elenn."

"The restoration is almost finished. I don't think I'll have any more spells like that," said Elenn. However, she knew there was no such assurance, and she knew that Hela was also quite aware of the fact. "If you really think it's best, I'll go along with whatever you say."

Hela said nothing. She was still walking with Elenn's arm up over her shoulder for support, as if Elenn needed help with walking. They both simultaneously realized that it wasn't necessary to walk that way any more because they were away from the gathering hall. They withdrew and looked briefly at each other.

"Master Hela," said Elenn in a low voice, "how can I thank you?" Master Hela looked at her kindly but said nothing. Elenn continued, "You have been so kind to me, even knowing that I am, … that I am … barren."

Hela looked at her with soft eyes of understanding before responding. "It only *happens* to be you who are barren," she said. "It only *happens* to be I who accompany you at this time. We are guard masters. Our life is directed at helping others through calamity and warding off misfortune however we can. I only wish I could do more for you."

They were still rather close to the outvillage, on a well-worn path that neither of them had previously explored. Suddenly they heard some high-pitched voices.

"It's the capital masters! Master Elenn! Master Hela!" It was the three child-uedin, running from behind them without any caretaker.

"The unnamed here are remarkably independent, aren't they?" commented Hela.

"Yes. I remember running off alone to do exercises when I was unnamed, but it wasn't until I was seven or eight. These are only four years old, and look how they run about."

The little unnamed came running with joyful excitement. "Master Elenn and Master Hela, are you going to look at the boiling muds?"

"The boiling muds? Are they near here?"

"Yes—they're right around that hill. Oh, wait till you see them!"

"All different colors!"

"Yes! Very pretty colors!" The child-uedin were full of chatter and excitement.

"But you have to be very careful because some of them are really boiling hot!"

"Not all of them."

"No, not all. Some of them are just warm. Sometimes Master Betol takes baths in the mud! Oh, you should see when she gets out—she's covered in mud all over!" The unnamed all giggled gleefully. Elenn thought to herself that the presence of child-uedin had a positive effect on her, and she felt as though she were completely recovered from the earlier mental confusion.

"She gets so dirty when she takes a bath in the mud!"

"Master Betol has such a big belly! When she takes a bath in the mud, she looks just like a big ball of mud!" They all squealed, stopping on the path to double over with laughter. Elenn and Hela exchanged a smile of amusement.

"There! There are the boiling muds!"

Elenn could smell them before she spotted them. After a few more steps she saw the steamy pockets, and then she saw a pool of liquid of a most unnatural color. It looked like a small pond of swirling pink and orange paint. Another small pool had a strange yellowish green color. The colors were indeed remarkable, just as the child-uedin had said.

"Very strange and beautiful, aren't they, Master Elenn?" murmured Hela quietly.

"Yes. I never imagined such a peculiar landscape."

There were quite a few mud pools. Some were obviously boiling and steaming, while others appeared to have completely cooled and hardened. The children ran ahead, tossing stones into the pools.

"Be careful now, unnamed! Don't go too close to them," warned Hela.

"We're fine—we do this all the time," one of them hollered back. The unfortunate aspect of the outvillage unnamed being so independent was that they did not appear to be nearly as obedient as Quarterhouse child-uedin. One of them took a stick and was poking it into the hardened crust of a cooled mud pool.

Suddenly Elenn heard what she first thought was a squeal of laughter but then recognized as screaming from one of the child-uedin. When she looked in the direction of the screams, she saw the little unnamed running toward them dropping her stick and waving her arms. The little one screamed in terror. It took a second or two to notice the strange grayish cloud that seemed to be surrounding her, then as the child-uedin approached, Elenn saw what it was, just as she heard Hela yell out.

"Wasps!"

The colony must have been enormous. The terrified little child-uedin brought the entire buzzing swarm directly to the rest of them. In seconds the noise became a loud drone that blocked out other sound. Elenn felt the first sting on her arm before she even considered how to react.

"Master Elenn! Guard the unnamed!" shouted Hela. Her voice sounded muted and faraway, as did the screams of the three child-uedin.

Elenn had to suppress instincts to fight and clear the wasps from her own face and body in order to direct her attention at helping the unnamed. They were screaming, jumping and waving their arms to rid themselves of wasps. One of them fell to the ground and kicked. Elenn could see the welts on her small legs and feet. As she rushed to grab the child-uedin, she saw Hela taking hold of another of them and holding her down, using her own body to shield her. Elenn saw that masses of wasps seemed to have landed on Hela's already swollen head and hands, crawling up her legs and under her sleeves.

The child-uedin in Elenn's arms screamed and choked, spitting out the wasps that crawled into her mouth. Elenn felt her own fingers swelling and stiffening with wasp stings, and her eyes were beginning to swell shut. The third child-uedin was not far from where Hela was lying on top of the other. She appeared to be disoriented, unable to see with eyes swollen shut, stumbling about with her arms outstretched.

"Master Hela!" Elenn struggled to call out. She could barely catch her breath enough to yell. "The other unnamed … right behind you!" A wasp flew into her mouth as she yelled. She felt its twitching legs and papery wings trying to buzz before she could spit it out. Hela didn't move. Elenn didn't know whether this meant she was unconscious or just couldn't hear. She wrapped the side of her guard's robe around the child-uedin in her arms as much as she could and hurried to get the other child-uedin. Wasps batted against her face and body as she ran. Her vision, already limited by the swelling of her eyelids, was crossed by the whizzing shapes of wasps coming right into her face. When she reached the child-uedin, the little one was no longer even trying to fight off the wasps. She could see the tails of wasps in both of the child's little nostrils. Her eyes were shut, and her screaming had turned into a listless whimpering. Elenn already had one child-uedin tucked under her arm beneath the flap of her guard's robe. She reached her right arm around the other and picked her up. A wasp trapped between the flesh of her arm and the skinny abdomen of the child-uedin vibrated and buzzed; it tickled and then stung her.

The first little one that she held with her left arm was still crying and kicking; the other under her right arm just hung there, gasping. These were lethal blue wasps. Once they swarmed, they did not stop stinging until their victims were dead. Elenn could hardly see, and from what she could make out there were two mud pools right ahead of them. She was going to have to jump into the hot mud with both child-uedin in order to escape them all being stung to death by the wasps. Both of the pools were steaming. There were two frightening possibilities if she were to jump in. One was that the mud would be boiling hot and kill them. The other was that the pool would be too deep and they would not be able to get out of it. The mud would be their refuge or it would be their grave. With eyes swollen and blurred vision, she could barely see at all, and having child-uedin in both arms, there was nothing to do but take a chance.

"Hold your breath, little one!" she shouted in the ear of the livelier of the two. She tried to hold her hand over the nose and mouth of the other one as her held her under her arm. She took five bounding strides and jumped with both child-uedin into one of the mud pools.

Elenn noticed a few wasps still pursuing them as they struck the surface. They all sunk in over their heads.

The burn of the hot mud instantly eclipsed the pain of wasp stings. She could see nothing, feel nothing but the burn. Only in the small areas where her arms were pressed against the flesh of the two little child-uedin did her skin burn less. She tried to kick to find a solid bottom with her feet. Her legs could not obey her because of the thickness of the hot mud. If she could reach something solid with her feet, she thought she might be able to push them all back up to the surface. No matter what, she must not let got of the two child-uedin in her arms. She stretched her legs to reach something solid—there was nothing but mud. She didn't know if the consistency of the mud was thin enough to let them float back up to the surface. She could hold her breath for a long period, but the child-uedin wouldn't be able to last very long. She held her hand tightly over the nose and mouth of the weakened child-uedin. The other one was starting to kick slowly against her in a fight for air. She clung to them both tightly. Finally she felt a ring of exposure at the top of her head where they were resurfacing. She pushed both child-uedin up to the air, which caused her own body to descend momentarily, but after a second or two she came up and took a gasp. She opened her eyes. Her vision was blurry as her eyes watered to cleanse out the mud that was in them, but she could see that the two unnamed were both at the surface and seemed to be struggling to keep themselves up. Their little heads and skullwombs were thickly coated with shiny bluish gray mud. Their eyes were still swollen shut. Their heads were completely covered with mud except for their little pink mouths as they panted for breath. With a few strokes of her arms, Elenn made her way to a spot in the pool where she could feel a solid surface under her feet. After she found something solid under one foot, she took a slow stride and found footing to step up on. Wasps were still swarming over them but did not attempt to sting through the thick coating of mud on their skin.

"Unnamed! Come this way!" Elenn shouted to the child-uedin, but they were confused and unable to move toward the sound of her voice. Elenn pushed herself back in toward them. As she moved, she tried to look out to see if there was any sign of movement from Hela, but from the pit of the mud pool she could not see anything in that direction. She reached the two unnamed. They were trying to kick and paddle in the thickness to keep themselves afloat. They coughed and cried—a good sign, she thought. She pulled them to herself and let them cling to her shoulders and then struggled through the mud to get back to the shallow spot.

The child-uedin sobbed quietly. She tried to comfort them. "We'll stay here till the wasps are gone. We'll be all right." One of them whimpered something, but Elenn couldn't make out what she was saying.

"What is it, little one?"

"Where is Crooked-tooth?"

Elenn thought for a moment and then remembered the nicknames of her own unnamed days at the Quarterhouse. Crooked-tooth had to be the name of the third unnamed. Hela still had her as far as she knew. The last thing she had seen of Hela was her lying on top of the other unnamed to shield her. She looked up and saw that Hela was still in the same spot.

"Master Hela!" she called out. The wasps were mostly gone now. It was quiet. "Master Hela!" There was no response.

Elenn made sure that the two unnamed she had with her in the mudpool were able to stand up on their own in the shallow area of the mud. Then she climbed out and up, and on to the bank. Now she could see the shape of Hela's body slumped across the smaller figure of the third child-uedin.

"Master Hela!" she called again. She ran to the spot where Hela had bent to shield the child-uedin with her own form. Hela had torn off her guard's robe and wrapped it around the child-uedin. Her entire body was covered with lumpy red welts. The wasps were gone except for the dead ones crushed in the struggle.

With her swollen and mud-covered hand Elenn reached down to Hela's shoulder and grasped it. She was afraid to see what she knew she was going to see. She yanked on Hela's body and turned her over. A few wasps flew out from underneath her. Two realities came to her at once: the movement of the child-uedin's form under the wrapping of Hela's guard's robe and the horrible frozen expression on the face of Hela's dead body. Hela's effort to shield the unnamed had succeeded, for even now the child-uedin was weakly tugging to pull the guard's robe from her head. But Hela's eyes, which had never swollen completely shut, were glazed over in death and her puffed face strained in an arrested attempt to draw air to her lungs. Her throat must have swollen shut, thought Elenn, and she had suffocated.

"Oh, Master Hela …" Emotion stole the sound from her voice.

She drew the guard's robe away. A few wasps were crawling slowly on the child-uedin's body. Elenn batted them away and lifted her up. She was badly stung and appeared to be semi-conscious but was breathing regularly. In her little open mouth Elenn could see her crooked tooth. She picked her up and walked back to the mud pool. The other two child-uedin were already hoisting themselves out of the mud.

"Master Elenn! What happened?!" A voice called out in alarm. It was Nehu. Other outvillage masters were right behind her. "What happened?"

Elenn could not speak. She looked back at the figure of her dead companion. Elenn had felt ashamed of many things during her life. At times she had felt terribly ashamed about her barren condition. At that moment she only felt ashamed that she had once considered the guardmasters to be unsophisticated and inferior. Master Hela had given everything and forfeited her own passing-of-life in service to the uedin. In Elenn's mind, there would never be any poet or scholar or temple server as decent and honorable as Master Hela.

Home from the Outvillage

Benar smiled into the floor as she snored lightly on her sleeping mat. The wheel-shaped pillow she rested her face on had shifted so that her nose was mashed against the side of it. In her dream, lovely little reed birds sang around her and billowy white clouds sailed overhead as she strode in great, sweeping, dancelike steps toward a shimmering turquoise lake. But then, there was something odd. The song of the reed birds turned into the noisy chirping of scavenger chicks.

With a jerk and a snort Benar woke herself and learned that the racket that had invaded her dream was coming from outside her window where scavenger chicks were apparently raiding the sourberry bushes. Then she remembered that she had left Master Elenn's new guard's robe in a boiling pot of green dye all night.

"Oh, no!" Benar leapt up and ran to the charcoal burner. The coals were burned down, but steam was still rising from the pot.

"What stupidity …" She picked up a large two-pronged fork and fished out the robe. Even if the color hadn't turned too dark, the cloth had probably shrunk. She lowered it into a bowl and carried it out the back entry. Then she opened it up and hung it over a tree limb. Steam rose against the cool morning air. It was just as she had feared—the robe had shrunk. Master Elenn had sewn it to replace the one that had been ruined, stained by some kind of mud, at Redrock outvillage. What terrible misfortune had occurred there. Elenn's poor comrade guard was stung to death by wasps—how terrible! When Elenn brought the new robe to ask Benar to dye it for her, Benar had tactfully stopped herself from commenting on its large size, realizing that Master Elenn was well into barren syndrome and already stood out among uedin. Instead, she quietly took the robe and told Elenn she would be glad to dye it for her, it was the least she could do. But now it had shrunk to a size more suited to a newly-named. What was she going to tell Master Elenn? Maybe she could stretch it out a bit while it was still wet.

She waited for it to cool enough to handle and then took it down from the limb, laid it out on the ground, and proceeded to tug at the ends of each sleeve. As she handled it, she noticed with regret that the robe had really been very beautifully sewn with exceptionally even stitching and careful work. Meanwhile, the dye covered her hands. She began to worry that she was going to get green dye on her own caretaker's robe. If the dye stained her skin, she could get most of it off in a bath, and the rest would wear off, but she certainly didn't want to get any permanent dye on her caretaker's robe. Better take her own robe off.

Sitting on the ground in her underwraps, Benar did her best to stretch out the wet, dye-soaked robe. At one point she tried to use her foot to pin one end down while she tugged on the collar to stretch it lengthwise. By the time she was done doing what she could do, her skin was stained here and there with splotches of green dye, especially her arms. She even had some green smudges on her face.

"Oh, what stupidity!" she said, and shook her head, looking at the oddly stretched robe lying on the ground. There wasn't any more she could do but give it a rinse, hang it up to dry, and let Master Elenn know that she needed to speak with her. After she had the robe rinsed and hanging over a branch, she wiped herself off the best she could, got her caretaker's robe from beneath the tree, and put it on carefully. Then she wrote a note to leave for Elenn at Flatpools Station and scurried off, hoping not to be seen with her green-stained arms. She would slip the note inside the door at Flatpools Station and go straight to the bathhouse.

That afternoon, Elenn walked from Flatpools station to Quarterhouse, still dazed from the tragedy at Redrock a few days earlier. There were actually two things weighing heavily on her. One was the death of Hela. The other was the obvious episodes of mental confusion that she had experienced, which she knew to be fits of derangement. Both tragic things made her very upset. She tried to concentrate on other things to help her stay focused. Her guard's garb had been ruined, stained in the mudpool, and she had spent the entire previous day sewing a new one out of white cloth and then taking it to Master Benar who had agreed to dye it for her. Benar had been functioning as her counselor for some time now. Elenn had known her since her unnamed times, and now Benar was one of the senior members of the new corps of specialty caretakers who worked specifically with uedin with barren syndrome. Elenn was initially embarrassed by the arrangement, but she liked Benar well enough. Benar provided information and practical recommendations without too much prying. She was glad that when she brought the new robe and asked Benar to dye it, Benar didn't question her about Hela, but only talked about the task at hand. Elenn explained that the guards generally ordered fabric from the capital textile masters once a novade when they received new recruits, but during off years the supply house was not restocked and the green cloth was hard to come by. Benar knew where to obtain green dye and said she would be glad to do it for her. That morning Elenn had received a message that Benar wanted her to come to her hut, so Elenn figured she must have finished the job.

One of the guards was coming her way on the path. It was Nemis.

"Getting back on track, Master Elenn?" asked the guard.

"Yes, as much as possible, thank you, Master Nemis," Elenn answered as good-naturedly as she was able. Everyone, it seemed, had heard some version of what had happened at

Redrock. *Good afternoon, Master Elenn ... Welcome home, Master Elenn ... You bring honor to the guard masters, Master Elenn.* Not only the guards—uedin she didn't even know who lived in the Flatpools District seemed to recognize her and insisted on making some sort of comment. But why did they really recognize her? Elenn did not want to be recognized this way, not by uedin who were aware of her condition and pitied her. She felt that the events at Redrock only gave them a comfortable excuse to direct their curiosity toward her. She did her best to nod and acknowledge them but was not inclined to engage in discussion with anyone.

She reached the Quarterhouse and made her way to Master Benar's hut. The door was open, tarp pulled aside and hooked up.

"Hello?" Elenn called in.

Master Benar came to the door. She had a large splotch of green color on her cheek. After a moment, Elenn noticed that her hands were also completely stained green.

"Master Benar, I had no idea that dyeing my guard robe was going to cause you this kind of inconvenience!"

"It's not your fault, Master Elenn. I'm afraid the dyeing operation did not go as well as I had hoped."

"Did you have an accident?"

"Well, I suppose you could say that I did have an accident, yes." Benar shook her head and looked down. "But really it was more of a simple case of stupidity."

"What happened?" asked Elenn.

Benar sighed with exasperation. "Last night I fell asleep and left your robe in the pot of dye on the charcoal stove—all night long!"

"You got some of the dye on your face and hands," said Elenn. "What happened?"

"Your robe shrunk. I tried to stretch it out while it was still wet." Benar had the most forlorn look on her face, but rather than conveying distress, it only looked comical on account of the stain on her cheek. She turned around to get the robe from a small table in the corner. "After stretching it the best I could, I rinsed it in cold water and dried it outside. Let's have a look." She handed the guard robe to Elenn. It was folded neatly. Elenn took hold of the collar lining and let it fall open. It was a brilliant shade of green, but it had obviously shrunk. Elenn took off the street garment she had worn from the station, put her arm into one the sleeves of the robe and drew it across her shoulders to put her other arm in the opposite sleeve. The sleeves fell barely below her elbows and pulled tight under her armpits.

"Not too bad," said Elenn. She turned toward Benar trying to look sincere, but she could not help cracking a smile.

"Oh Master Elenn," said Benar, "I wanted very much to do you a favor, but I don't think I've helped at all."

"Master Benar, you have gone to much trouble for me. It is not necessary to feel that way. Look—you've gotten green dye on yourself for my sake."

"Can you get more undyed cloth? Perhaps we can try again."

PUREST EXERCISE

Elenn didn't really see any alternative. "I'm sure Master Wanba will let me take whatever I need."

"I'm sorry you're going to have to take the time to sew it all again. Your stitching is very thorough. I'm sure it's time-consuming."

"It won't be any difficulty for me, Master Benar, thanks for your concern, but I hate to put you through the inconvenience of dyeing another one."

"I'll be more careful next time." Benar smiled with embarrassment, which Elenn noticed. She like the quality in Benar that was easily embarrassed and self-conscious. Even if it was somewhat humiliating for an adult uedin to be placed in the counsel of a caretaker of the unnamed, Elenn was glad that Benar had found her way to the position. When no amount of thinking was going to solve a situation, a kind heart was the best qualification.

"How is your foot, Master Elenn?" asked Benar.

"My foot?" Elenn was perplexed.

"Yes… I saw the report from Redrock. The trouble all started when you stepped on a poison thistle?"

The outvillagers had provided a full report of incidents related to Hela's death that was sent along with a few outvillagers who accompanied Elenn and transported the body back to the capital. Apparently Deben or Wanba or someone had chosen to let Benar see the report.

Elenn hesitated about the poison thistle. Benar didn't wait for Elenn's answer, shook her head and commented, "I've heard that the poison thistle can be very debilitating. I'm glad we don't have them around the capital."

Elenn looked down at the folded robe in her hands. It was a brilliant color. It was pity that she wouldn't be able to wear it, but if she lasted long enough, there might be a trainee after the next Namesgiving to whom she might be able to pass it on.

"There was no poison thistle," said Elenn.

"You didn't step on a poison thistle?" asked Benar.

"Master Benar, I've been having …" the weight of the topic seemed to rise inside her, pushing emotion up into her chest. "I've been having some kind of spells."

"Yes," said Benar looking at her seriously and waiting for more explanation. But Elenn didn't explain, and Benar already knew what she was talking about. "You had a spell like that when you were in Redrock?"

"I became very confused." Elenn's voice was suddenly high pitched and tensed as she tried to suppress the emotion.

"So, you had a spell while you were at the outvillage. The outvillagers thought you had stepped on a poison thistle." Benar politely ignored Elenn's emotion.

"Yes." Elenn's eyes started to tear up, but she tried to stay cool. She told Benar about how the outvillagers had thought that Elenn must have stepped on a poison thistle, and Hela had gone along with it, to protect her. She told her about the wasps, even though Benar had already read the report. By this time she had quieted her emotions. She said calmly, "It was because of me that Master Hela lost her passing-of-life."

Benar looked back at her quizzically. "No, Master Elenn, Master Hela sacrificed her passing to save the child-uedin of the outvillage. You must know how grateful the outvillage is for the rescue of their child-uedin. Can you imagine how devastating it would have been for them if they had lost their only three unnamed all at once?" Elenn knew the truth of this. But would the child-uedin have been playing around the mud pools if they had not spotted Hela and herself in that area? There was no way of knowing, but she couldn't help feeling that there was a connection between the tragedy of Hela's death and her own condition, which was the real reason why they had walked from the restoration project site. Whether there was direct responsibility or not, feelings of shame persisted. She thought about the night they had camped in the salt flats before they reached Redrock. She had been helplessly attracted to the skullsap vein on the back of Master Hela's neck. Now Hela was dead, and deprived of her passing.

"I know I played a part," said Elenn flatly. The look in her eye told Benar that she was not looking for Benar to try to disagree or reassure her.

Benar frowned and shook her head. "Master Elenn, the spell you had was not something you had in your control. You have controlled yourself very steadfastly. There are other barren uedin who are not nearly as able to control themselves as you are. You're only a second-generation uedin. You still have time. You're still very healthy."

"I'm sorry. I don't see how anyone can regard me as being healthy." This much, Elenn said out loud. She did not mention the other thoughts that came into her head. She did not mention that the picture of that dreadful barren she had seen in the lichen field when she was newly-named. She did not mention that she feared, more than anything, becoming like that, nor that what she really wanted was to die, that she wished it had been she that died at Redrock instead of Hela.

"Master Elenn, I am going to tell you something confidential." Benar's voice lowered, suggesting that what she had to say was serious and not public knowledge. "I've heard that they've been talking about a new plan on the council. The medic masters know that a lot of the symptoms of barren syndrome are caused by skullsap that gets circulated back into the body instead of going to the embryo."

"That's been known. They were already saying that when I received my diagnosis." Elenn thought about her own vacant skullwomb with no embryo to receive the sap. Her skullwomb rested empty on the back of her head where she was aware of it every minute of every day.

"But now the medic masters are experimenting with the idea of draining skullsap out of the body."

Elenn had actually wondered herself if such a thing might one day be attempted. "How would they do this? Would they call us regularly to the infirmary to have it bled from us?"

"I don't know the details, but I believe they are testing a device that would enable the excess skullsap to drain."

Elenn tried to imagine such a thing. The picture disgusted her. "What, would it just drain out all the time? Would it drain into some kind of vessel?"

"I imagine so, something that could be emptied regularly."

"This is being discussed at council meetings?"

"It is. If it works, it won't undo any barren syndrome, it won't give you an embryo, but it will enable you to live without the symptoms, without derangement. It might stop the physical overdevelopment too—if started early enough." Obviously in Elenn's case it would not be early enough.

Elenn looked seriously at Benar's face. This was indeed a major development. If it were true, this could change her life completely.

"But then what would happen to us?"

"What would happen to you?" Benar didn't understand what Elenn was inquiring about. "Well, I suppose you would live and serve in the capital." She said, nodding cluelessly.

"But how would it end? We still would have no passing-of-life." Uedin with barren syndrome were not known to live longer than four generations, so there had never been any question about how the life of barren uedin would conclude if it were to extend into ro age.

"You're quite right," Benar said thoughtfully. "I'm sure the council is discussing that. The important thing is that a treatment may become available for the symptoms. I say *may* become available, now—I really don't know for sure."

"How do you know about it at all, Master Benar? Did you get some communication from the council?"

"No ..." Benar shook her head and looked down with regret, as if she now realized she shouldn't have brought it up at all. "I heard something about it from one of the other caretakers in the corps. I probably shouldn't have mentioned it, but I wanted to give you something to hope for."

Elenn didn't know whether she would even want to live a long time with her barren condition and no passing-of-life at the end. Benar only knew a little bit, just what she had heard. Who would be able to give her more information about this? She immediately thought of Master Domas. Master Domas was once on the council, and she would probably know more. Master Domas had been her advisor. Master Domas would tell her the truth.

"Is Master Domas still on the masters council?" asked Elenn.

"Oh, no. She relinquished her position some time ago. Master Domas is, um …" Benar smiled vacantly and brushed some crumbs off the table top. "Master Domas is preparing for her pilgrimage now." Elenn knew what this was supposed to mean. Master Domas was losing her mental faculties—entering ro ecstasy.

"Pilgrimage—already? Isn't Master Domas only in her ninth generation?"

"No, it's her tenth now. Domas is four generations ahead of me."

"Even tenth—that's early for a passing."

Benar nodded and smiled knowingly, showing her familiarity with this point. "Master Domas has always been early at everything. She was known for having been ahead of her peers when she studied the codes to become a teaching master, and then she took on responsibilities in the Quarterhouse sooner than the masters usually do. She's always been in a hurry somehow." Benar shrugged. "And so it seems fitting that she will be the first of her generation to depart for her pilgrimage."

"Is she receiving any visitors?"

"Oh, I don't think so, Master Elenn." Benar sighed and looked down dismissively. "Master Domas is really quite advanced into her ecstasy. Why do you want to see her?"

"I think Master Domas will remember me. I want to ask her what she knows about this plan to treat barren syndrome."

"But I don't think it's a plan, it's probably only a consideration at this point. It's not supposed to be public knowledge yet. I only told you because I thought it might help you. I wanted you to see that things may not be as bad as they seem. But I happen to know that Master Domas isn't in the right state of mind to receive a visitor."

Who else *was* there? What would it mean to Elenn if her life were to be extended indefinitely, long novades ahead of her leading to nothing? She had to know whether she might have to face such a fate, but Domas was the only uedin she knew who might know something more than hearsay. Would Master Benar try to discourage Elenn from visiting Master Domas just to avoid being scolded for giving out secret information? Elenn thought she might. Domas had great influence in the capital. Benar probably didn't want Domas thinking poorly of her.

"I do appreciate your confidence Master Benar. It's true what you say—things may not be as bad as they seem." Silently she thought to herself that things could just as easily be even worse.

"You're a fine young guard master. That's the most important thing."

Elenn drew her hands to her face and signified that she was going to take her leave. "Well, Master Benar, please allow me to excuse myself. Everything you've said has been quite true and very helpful."

"Yes, good then! You must hold your head high! You bring honor to the guard masters—don't deny them the chance to be proud of you!"

Elenn thought this was absurd, but she appreciated the words. "Thank you, Master Benar."

"And you'll bring me your new robe for dyeing."

"I will." Elenn hoped that she could depend on Benar not to shrink it again.

"I'll see you again soon then, Master Elenn."

"Again soon," said Elenn. Leaving the caretaker hut, she glanced back to see Benar scratching her behind with a green-stained hand. Instead of heading back toward the station, Elenn cut across the Quarterhouse grounds toward Domas's old residence.

A Visit to Master Domas

A young caretaker was hunched down, scraping the bottom of a burned pan with a piece of wire mesh outside of Domas's entranceway.

"Good afternoon, Master," said Elenn.

The caretaker looked up, squinting into the sun. "Good afternoon, Master," she answered. She saw the green folded guard's robe in Elenn's hands. Was this master from the guard's station, she wondered. "Has there been any trouble?"

"No. I'm here to pay a visit to Master Domas."

The caretaker stood up. As soon as she stood, she took notice of Elenn's tallness. A complexity of reaction showed on her face. Suspicion, pity, repulsion, compassion, curiosity. She was speaking to a barren.

"Is Master Domas expecting you?"

"No, master, she is not expecting me. Is it better if I come at another time?"

The caretaker continued to gaze at her as though looking at something strange. "What is your name, Master?"

"I am Elenn of the capital guards, Flatpools District. I am also an alumnus of Quarterhouse."

The young caretaker seemed troubled, reluctant to let Elenn meet with the ro-master.

Elenn persisted. "Master Domas was my tutor, and later my advisor when I was newly-named."

The caretaker had a strange look of doubt on her face. Perhaps, thought Elenn, she never imagined that a barren would have an ordinary life history. "Wait here just a moment please, Master," said the caretaker and disappeared inside Domas's residence. Elenn heard her speaking to Master Domas in a loud and slow voice. She couldn't hear Domas's voice, but she must have asked a lot of questions because the caretaker repeated Elenn's name and information numerous times. Finally she came out and said, "Please go in." Then she added, "Master Domas is not at her best, you know."

Elenn found Domas sitting at a small table with four small bowls and a large bunch of currants. She was counting and dividing the currants into the four bowls.

"One, two, three, four, one, two, three, four, one, two …"

"Master Domas, it's been a very long time!" Elenn raised hands to face.

" …four, one, two, three, four …" Domas looked up for just an instant but continued counting.

"Do you remember me, Master Domas? I'm Elenn. You were my counselor before the end of the last novade."

Domas stopped abruptly and looked at her. "Elenn?" she said, repeating the name she had just heard.

"Yes." Elenn smiled politely. She still was not sure she was being recognized.

"*Streetsweeper bending in the fog, picking willow twigs out of the dust, when she has enough, then a tiny fire, when she has enough, then a short rest, a chance to warm her fingers.* Name the poet and context."

Elenn took a deep breath. Domas was quizzing her. Perhaps it was her way of meeting her old students with nostalgia. Elenn remembered once knowing that verse, but she couldn't recall anything about it. She laughed nervously. "Are you quizzing me, Master Domas? It's been a very long time since I reviewed any of the verses or codes."

Then Domas laughed hard. "You're Elenn, right? You wanted to be a server but instead you joined the capital guards!" Elenn was relieved to be recognized, but also taken aback by Domas's brusqueness.

"Yes," replied Elenn quietly, "I am the one you're talking about."

"You see? You see, young Master Yenca?" She called out to the caretaker standing at the doorway. "I do remember! I do remember a thing or two!"

"Of course you do, Master Domas," said the caretaker.

Elenn had seen rapid change come over ro-uedin before when they entered their phase of ecstasy for the passing. But this was Master Domas. She never imagined Master Domas losing her mental clarity.

Domas continued talking to the caretaker. She pointed at Elenn. "This guard master wanted to be a server, but she joined the capital guards instead." Elenn knew that Master Domas was only smiling because she was pleased with her own ability to remember. She was not trying to be cruel. Then Domas looked at Elenn straight in the eye with a look of exaggerated pity.

"It's too late, you know," she said. "Too late to be a server." She shook her head sadly. "You can't change your mind now. You'll have to stay in the guards."

"I know that, Master Domas. I don't want to be a server any more. I'm glad to be a capital guard."

"Yes, you should be. The capital guards serve a vital function. Don't they, Master Yenca? Don't the capital guards serve a vital function?"

"Indeed they do," said Yenca. She was used to having to give Domas an affirmation for every little thing.

Elenn had a sinking feeling in her chest. She wished she hadn't come to visit Master Domas now. Master Benar wasn't trying to steer her away to save her own reputation—Master Domas really was into her ro ecstasy. It didn't look as though she was going to get any valuable information about the council's plans to treat barren syndrome. She wasn't sure if it was even worth asking about.

"You wouldn't have liked being a server." She tapped her forehead. "Because you're a *thinker*!" She laughed with self-satisfaction at this analysis. "We masters are thinkers! That's why we can't tend the Lern Beyana because our minds are too *busy*!" She laughed again. "What do you think, Master Yenca, isn't it true?"

"Very true, Master Domas, very perceptive." The caretaker's manner seemed condescending to Elenn.

"Master Domas, do you still have any connection with the masters council?" Elenn decided it would not hurt to ask.

"Of course!" barked Domas. She seemed indignant at the notion that anyone would consider otherwise. "I'm a senior member of the council!"

Yenca looked at Elenn out of the corner of her eye and shook her head very slightly to suggest that it was not true.

"But I can't change the rules for you! You have to stay in the guards!"

"I know that Master Domas—"

"A uedin can't say she's going to be a master one day and then decide she wants to be a server instead!" Domas seemed to be getting very agitated.

"Of course not, Master Domas, I wasn't trying—"

"You made your choice!" Domas banged her fist on the table with great force. One of the bowls of currants bounced and toppled onto the floor. Domas sat on her bench for a moment, looking down and assessing the situation. The currants had spilled and rolled around Domas's feet. Yenca moved in to help pick them up.

"Oh—try not to crush them," said Domas, and she bent to pick some up. Elenn put the folded guard's robe she was carrying off to the side and tried to help. As she reached around,

Domas, who had said not to crush them, absently picked up her feet and put them down, crushing currants into purple stains on the floor planks.

"Just sit back, Master Domas," said Yenca. "We'll pick them all up for you. We'll wash them, and they'll be fine."

Domas ignored her and kept on crushing more than she was picking up. "Oh, I was dividing these to share with my friends," she lamented.

"You still can. There's plenty," said Yenca. Elenn was on her knees trying to pick up the currants around Domas's feet.

When Domas reached down in front of her, Elenn's hand was positioned for an instant right beside her own. That is when she saw that Elenn's hand was larger than her own hand, and too large to be the hand of a normal uedin. Elenn heard her gasp, and then felt Domas's bony fingers clutch her wrist.

"Your hand!" she said. And then she looked up into Elenn's face with surprise. She let go and stood up, knocking the stool out from under her. Now she saw that Elenn was much taller than her as well.

"You're—you're barren!"

Elenn gently let the small handful of currants drop into the bowl and stepped back. She lowered her eyes and said nothing.

"She's barren, isn't she, Master Yenca?"

"I was afraid of this," Yenca said to Elenn quietly. "Master Domas has had nightmares of being attacked by a—master with the syndrome. She has an irrational fear. Perhaps it would be best for you to go."

"I know what you want!" Domas cried out and held her hands to the back of her neck to protect it.

"I had no idea," said Elenn to Yenca. She reached for the folded robe. Domas stood with her back to the wall, terrified.

"I'm very sorry," said Yenca. "I should have explained earlier."

"It's all right. I'm going." Elenn walked out swiftly. She was stunned by what had happened. She walked back to the station, feeling strangely outside of herself.

Treatments Begin in the Capital

Within a shorter moon cycle, Elenn received notification that she would be eligible for a new, experimental treatment. A few days later, she was in the station when a team of distributor masters came with a food delivery. One of the masters who happened to be walking alongside the cart, checking off items as they were delivered, was wearing some sort of bandage on the back of her neck. She wasn't particularly tall or exceptional looking. Elenn would not initially have thought she was barren if it weren't for the bandage. But once it caught her attention, Elenn picked up on a certain glum detachment that made her feel certain that the distributor master was another one like herself. After that, she began to see them around the capital. Some had obvious bandages and others seemed to have some kind of strap that ran up from the collar of their robes. Elenn made no effort to contact the infirmary for an appointment. When she received a notice to see Master Wanba, she had a hunch that Wanba was going to try to persuade her to accept treatment. She found Master Wanba and Master Henik reviewing census records in the station that afternoon.

"Please pardon my interruption, masters," said Elenn. "Master Wanba, I received this note to see you …" she held the paper up.

"Oh, yes," said Wanba. "Master Elenn, please come in." They were working on the floor. She put another sitting pad on the floor mat. "Please."

Elenn sat down with her senior guards. They were drinking cups of milkgrass tea. Henik poured some for Elenn.

Wanba spoke directly. "Master Elenn, we all know you're struggling with your condition, and we know Master Hela's death was very terrible for you." Elenn knew that when Wanba said *all*, she wasn't exaggerating. All the guard masters at Flatpools knew about her. Wanba continued, "There will be a memorial service for Master Hela after the equinox, and you will be expected to take part in the tribute. Your involvement in the rescue of the child-uedin from the outvillage will also be awarded. You will have to appear for public recognition."

"I see." said Elenn. "Thank you for giving me advance notice."

Henik spoke next. "You may have heard, Master Elenn, there is a new treatment being provided to uedin with the syndrome. You may want to consider moving ahead with your own treatment in time to have the implant heal before your appearance."

So, thought Elenn, that's why some of the individuals she saw had bandages and others had the strap extending up from their collars. The bandages were necessary while implants healed. She had procrastinated making an appointment at the infirmary. Why extend life as a barren? It was awful to know that one was going to deteriorate, but at least it shortened the length of a barren life. What uedin would really want to live long with no passing-of-life ahead of her? But Elenn had never voiced these thoughts, not with Master Benar who was there to guide her, and certainly not with her fellow guards. How could the medic masters just assume that uedin with barren syndrome would want their treatment?

Being careful not to sound too much as though she were protesting, Elenn said, "I would like to know how others like myself feel about a treatment of symptoms that could result in a long future with no passing-of-life."

Henik and Wanba both stared at Elenn, momentarily taken aback. Dismay gradually registered on their faces. Wanba looked a little impatient; Henik was the more sympathetic of the two. Elenn had never spoken of her condition to Henik, but she had the feeling that Henik understood her difficulty to some degree. She wished she could just speak openly. *Masters, if you were going to have no passing-of-life, would you want to live a long time?* She felt it would be too defiant a thing to say, but as she thought it, she caught a look in Henik's eyes that made her feel as though Henik was already thinking about the same thing.

Wanba was better prepared to present some no-nonsense direction. "What choice do you have, Master Elenn?" she asked sternly.

Elenn considered her choice of words before answering, and then spoke softly. "I've always thought I would do as earlier uedin with barren syndrome have done. I'd leave the capital when it became necessary to do so, and I would face my end in the wilderness."

Wanba looked at Henik to see whether she could count on her to support her in argument, but Henik did not look up. Elenn felt grateful. She was consoled to think that Henik understood her feelings.

Wanba spoke directly. "Even though you are only into your first novade with the guards, you've seen enough to know what the barren syndrome does. There would be nothing but misery in such a choice. How would it be if a guard master, charged with the protection of uedin, became a danger?"

"Because I am a guard, I will be among other guard masters who are prepared to do what is necessary to protect the capital," answered Elenn quietly. "If I cannot myself ascertain when it is time to depart the capital, the guards will tell me."

"I think it would be complicated, Master Elenn. The guards have been tested hard with trouble from barren uedin. They may not be as helpful as you imagine. Or, on the other hand, they might be too interested in trying to protect you, pretending that you're fine and hiding you. It will become the responsibility of us senior guards to watch you, which is something we don't have time for. It would be better for all of us if you would accept treatment."

Elenn had, up to this point, maintained a cool composure. But as she began to understand that she was going to be forced to accept treatment, and thus forced to live many generations with her condition, she had to fight to keep her face from knotting up with emotion.

"I understand," she said in a strained voice. She rose to leave.

"Wait!" Henik stopped her. "Master Wanba, if I am willing to take responsibility for monitoring Master Elenn and giving her instruction, and even taking her out of the capital myself when the time comes, would you consider allowing her to decide this matter on her own?"

Wanba looked at Henik with mild irritation. She clearly didn't like the idea, but she found it too awkward to refuse Henik's suggestion. She sighed with resignation, and Elenn felt great relief. Wanba was not going to insist on her getting the implant. "We choose our own name, and our own work here in the capital," Wanba finally said. "Elenn will not be forced to accept treatment against her will as long as she demonstrates a sound mind."

Henik nodded in appreciation to Wanba. She was also nodding to indicate that she understood the responsibility she was accepting. She spoke seriously to Elenn. "Master Elenn, I can't know what's best. Please do what you must. I will observe as much as I can and speak often with your fellow guards. If you choose not to receive treatment, I will do my best to take action when it becomes no longer suitable for you to remain in the capital."

Elenn had not expected such a generous empathy from Master Henik. She lowered her head and brought hands to face in gratitude. "I have no words to thank you for this kindness, Master Henik," she said. "But I will also consider the recommendation of Master Wanba. I would never want to risk bringing any dishonor to the guards."

"We will look forward to your appearance at Master Hela's memorial service."

"Yes, Master," said Elenn. "Thank you for the tea."

As she was leaving the guard station, she saw Master Simol. Now that Master Hela was gone, Simol was the only other guard in Elenn's generation who had come with her from Quarterhouse. Simol and Hela had been close ever since they had taken name. Elenn, preoccupied with her own situation, had never minded being the outsider. Elenn suspected that Simol had learned about her condition at some early point and had always been somewhat uncomfortable with her. But now they had grieving Hela's death in common, and they had spoken a few times with a new openness.

"Hello, Master Simol."

"Master Elenn, I've been looking for you. What is your assignment for tomorrow?" she asked.

"I've been given street inspections every day. I don't believe there's been any change," said Elenn.

"The Bells masters are working on some Equinox preparations, and they're sending their unnamed to play at the peat moss beds tomorrow. Master Nemis and I were asked to chaperone, but Master Nemis is looking for someone to trade with her. She doesn't want to get home late because she's in the middle of a big project—making yeastdrink, actually." Simol laughed.

"Well, if Master Nemis doesn't mind doing the street inspections, I'd be happy to go along with you," said Elenn. She had not been to the peat moss beds since she was unnamed herself. "Do we need approval from one of the senior guards?"

"Master Deben got approval for us. I think she wants some of the yeastdrink." Simol smiled.

There was a concern that needed to be acknowledged. Elenn decided she would bring it to the open. "Master Simol, I will have to ask one favor of you."

"Yes, Master?"

She didn't quite know how to express her concern. "If I seem to act strangely in any way …"

Simol nodded and quickly interrupted, "Of course I will be there to help you if you have any problems, Master Elenn. I'll be very direct with you if anything seems wrong."

The quick response gave Elenn mixed feelings. Simol and Deben had obviously already discussed the possibility that she could have one of her spells. She didn't like being talked about, even if it was necessary. But she needed to smile and appear to be of good cheer. "Good then," she said, "It sounds like a nice outing."

"A very pleasant assignment," said Simol. "The Bells unnamed are a small group. There are only twenty or so."

"See you in the morning then, Master Simol."

"In the morning, Master Elenn."

Elenn could barely remember playing at the peat moss beds in her early childhood. It was going to be very pleasant to go there again.

At the Peat Moss Beds

Bells was the name of a school and domicile in the northwest part of the capital where a small group of unnamed were trained in basic skills. It took its name from the two graceful bell towers that marked its otherwise undistinguished architecture. If Bells had neither an impressive edifice nor prestigious archives, it did have splendid wooden cabinets and tapestries. It was known for providing the capital with many of its carpenters and weavers.

Bells had just two caretakers. They had received a letter from a third-generation guard, a Master Deben, who explained that one of the guards being sent to chaperone had barren syndrome, but that the other guard was well prepared and would be there at all times in case of any difficulties. They were both waiting with child-uedin in the early morning fog when Simol and Elenn arrived at their gate.

"If you're very polite, the guard masters might play with you when you get to the peat moss beds!" said one of the caretakers to the child-uedin with a smiling glance toward Simol and Elenn. Elenn knew that her size was an immediate giveaway of her condition and was both puzzled and relieved that the caretaker did not appear to be afraid of her. The unnamed regarded them both with wide-eyed curiosity, more fascinated with the presence of capital guards than anything else. The other caretaker came to speak with Simol and Elenn. She wore a more serious expression.

"Masters, one of our unnamed is blind. She will need assistance if she goes along to the peat moss beds. Would it be best if we kept her at Bells?"

Simol and Elenn looked at the group of child-uedin to see if they could tell which one it was. They saw her, facing her head in a different direction from the others who were all still silently admiring their guards robes.

"She can certainly come along," said Simol, exchanging a glance with Elenn to make sure they agreed.

"Thank you, masters," said the caretaker. "We've packed baskets with some food—melonseed buns and rivergrapes, enough for everyone. The unnamed can help you carry them."

The child-uedin walked in single file after Elenn. The blind child-uedin kept her place perfectly well by listening to the footsteps of the one in front of her. Simol followed at the back of the line.

Once they were outside the capital walls, sunlight began to break through the fog. The unnamed relaxed and started to chatter and laugh. Elenn's heart was cheered by the golden morning sun and sound of their carefree voices. The road that led to the peat moss beds turned off from the North Route and led through a stretch of lowland shrubs, now yellow from the colder nights as the three-quarter equinox was but days away. Simol spotted two large anteaters rummaging in the weeds, and they all stopped for a while to watch in fascination. Elenn noticed the blind child-uedin cocking her head in case she might hear some sound from them.

The unnamed cheered and ran ahead when they reached the peat moss beds. Over the centuries, peat had been periodically cut for fuel when cold seasons were particularly cold and other sources of heat ran low. But the beds had been untouched for a number of generations and were thick with new growth. The result was a bowl of hodgepodge terraces that formed a soft and bouncy playground for jumping and tumbling. The moss was dry from the long summer and perfect for play.

At first, a few of the unnamed kept company with the blind child-uedin who was less able to frolic. But soon they innocently ran off to join in games and races, leaving her alone to feel about cautiously. Simol played with the more rambunctious ones. Elenn kept company with the little blind child-uedin. She took her to a spot where the peat terraces formed a giant stairway and helped her climb to the top. There they sat and rested, enjoying the warmth of the sun and listening to the noise below.

"What school did you come from, Master?" asked the child-uedin.

"I'm from Quarterhouse," answered Elenn.

"Oh, Quarterhouse," said the child-uedin. "You must know lots of verses."

"Yes, I know hundreds of them," said Elenn.

"Tell me a verse."

Elenn tried to think of something suitable. She thought of one that had the word 'bells' in it.

"All right—here's a verse written by a server. She lived long ago, and she liked riddles.

> *Fluttering feathers back and forth*
> *Swinging bells back and forth*
> *All things reaching back and forth*
> *They always reach for me.*
> *Who am 'I'?"*

The blind child-uedin smiled ticklishly. "No, I don't know. What is it?"

"Are you sure? Think about it," said Elenn. She repeated the verse.

"I don't know what it is, but I like the part about the bells!"

"Well now, that's right, your school is Bells, isn't it!" She waited a minute to see if the child-uedin could figure out the riddle, then gave the answer.

"Shall I tell you? All right … it's *gravity*!" said Elenn.

"Oh yes, *gravity*!" said the unnamed with excitement. "*Gravity*." She said it again, proud of knowing the word. It was a big word for a small child-uedin, but she knew what it meant. "That's a very clever riddle!" She reached her little hand over and patted Elenn on the arm. "Tell me another one!"

"Why don't you tell me one?"

"I don't know any verses."

"You know one, at least, don't you?"

"No ... I don't know any verses at all."

The bowl-shaped pit of moss beds had the strange effect of muffling sound. From where Elenn and the blind child-uedin sat, noise of the play below was so muted that only sudden peals of laughter stood out against the sound of the breeze in the shrubs.

"No, I don't know any verses at all." The child-uedin turned her head and listened. She thought she might be able to know what games they were playing if she could hear them. She could not. She said quietly, "I know how to weave. I'm good at weaving." She did not seem to be particularly excited about her ability to weave.

"That's a wonderful skill," said Elenn. "That's something I don't know at all!"

The child-uedin accepted this encouragement. "I know a song."

"Why don't you sing a song then? Sing a song for me!"

The child-uedin stood up to sing. It was how the Bells masters had taught her.

> *"Hokey pokey turtle in her turtle shell*
> *When the puppy comes she does very well*
> *Just take a nap and when she wakes up*
> *No more sign of the naughty little pup!"*

"That was wonderful!" said Elenn.

"Our tutors and caretakers at Bells sing that to us sometimes," said the child-uedin with pride.

"Well, I think they must be very fine masters," said Elenn. "Sing it again and I'll try to sing along."

They began together, *"Hokey pokey turtle in her turtle shell, When the puppy comes she does very well—"*

Elenn's voice stopped. The child-uedin sang a few more words and then stopped as well.

"What's the matter?" asked the child-uedin.

"I see something over on the hill."

"Is it an anteater?" The child had not been able to stop remembering the anteater, unable to imagine what sort of creature it might be.

"No," said Elenn. "it's a uedin."

Off in the distance there was bare hill of rock protruding from the brush. A uedin was there, stripped to her underwrappings, and doing a shifting exercise. What appeared to be a medic master's robe was folded on the ground beside her.

"What is the uedin doing?"

"She is doing a shifting exercise." Elenn watched as the uedin swung from position to position with great strength and poise. It came to her that the figure was quite large. Could she be barren? Elenn stood to get a better look. The figure bent forward. Elenn could see the strap that ran the length of her neck. She *was* barren!

"Is she very skilled at shifting?" asked the child-uedin.

"Yes. Her skill is really quite remarkable." Elenn was transfixed. She had seen server demonstrations of shifting that were far more advanced. But it wasn't the actual shifting that impressed Elenn so much as the stunning image of so large a figure—large as only a barren can be—directing her mass with such grace and discipline. It seemed like an image from a dream. As she watched the stranger shift, Elenn felt something shifting inside herself. The uedin dignity, the integrity, that had always seemed impossible, unreachable to her, was here manifest before her eyes by this stranger who obviously bore her same condition. She had learned when she herself was unnamed: "Our lives bear meaning by the lives we bear." Now a lesson was coming to her that told her—*Our lives bear meaning, no matter what.* She looked at the little blind child-uedin beside her, innocently turning her head about as if she might actually hear some sound generated by the distant shifting. She was suddenly filled with a wave of appreciation for the preciousness of the blind child-uedin with her turtle song, experiencing life from her special place. *Our lives bear meaning in the songs we sing,* she thought. *Our lives bear meaning in the riddles we tell ... the courage we find, the struggles we accept ...* Elenn's eyes filled with tears.

"If she's very good, then she must be pleasing to Lern Beyana," said the child-uedin.

"Yes, little one," said Elenn with deep emotion. "I feel sure that she is."

Ro-uedin Bid Farewell to One Departing For Her Pilgrimage

Lemeh and Hera stood at the Northgate with a lit lantern, sacks of food, and some gourds of water, waiting for Domas to appear with her caretaker. It was just getting dark, and the lantern cast a shadow on the wall of the gate's stone arch.

"There would be many here to send off Master Domas if she had wanted to let them all come," said Lemeh.

"Oh, there would be a crowd," agreed Hera, "but Domas didn't want them."

"And she didn't want Master Gisef to come," added Lemeh.

"Master Gisef says outlandish things," commented Hera, "and maybe Master Domas didn't want to hear such things when she was leaving for her pilgrimage."

"Well, that is her right. It is her departure for her pilgrimage, and if she doesn't want Master Gisef coming to bid her farewell, she does not have to invite her," said Lemeh.

"Yes, you are correct," said Hera, nodding reassuringly, "she doesn't have to if she doesn't want to. And if she doesn't want a crowd, she doesn't have to have one."

"We are the only ones here," said Lemeh. "I wonder if we are the only ones who will bid farewell to Master Domas."

"If that is the case, it is our honor," said Hera.

"Yes, indeed, it is a great honor," said Lemeh.

"Perhaps she honors us because we are older than her. We are in our eleventh novade, and she is only in her tenth," said Hera.

"It's true. And Master Gisef is her same age. Master Gisef is just in her tenth," said Hera.

"It is unusual to go to one's passing of life during one's tenth novade. Master Domas was always the first at everything. And she is the first of her generation to go to her passing. Imagine! She is going to her passing-of-life before us, even though we are eleventh generation and she is only tenth!" said Lemeh.

"Yes, it is remarkable," said Hera. "But soon it will be our turn. Who do you think will go first, Master Lemeh? Will it be you or I?"

"I don't know, but if it is I who go first, I hope you will come to bid me farewell," said Lemeh.

"And if it is *I* who go first, I hope you will come to bid *me* farewell," answered Hera.

"But we will not go at the same time," added Lemeh with great seriousness.

"Oh no, we will not go at the same time. Because one must go on her pilgrimage alone. It is the proper way to go to one's passing-of-life."

"Yes of course," agreed Lemeh. "We will leave on separate occasions for separate pilgrimages."

Suddenly they saw another lantern coming toward them. It was Yenca, carrying a lantern with one hand and holding the hand of Domas with the other.

Domas was whispering to herself, "How does it go? *Happy the bones, there in the lake …*"

" *'there in the sweet pool,'*" corrected Yenca.

"… *there in the lake,*" Domas ignored her, "*happy stars, …*"

" *'White under the stars,'* " said Yenca.

"*And singing, singing, singing, singing, singing, singing!*" sang Domas.

"Oh, hello masters. Thank you for coming," said Yenca to Hera and Lemeh.

"The stars are singing!" said Domas.

"We're very honored to be here. Aren't we Master Lemeh?"

"Oh yes," said Lemeh, "very honored! Thank you for letting us come, Master Domas."

But Domas was oblivious to their presence. "I am leaving! The time has come, and I am leaving!"

"Yes, Master Domas," said Yenca gently and kindly. "Your time has come, and we will miss you, but we are happy for you."

Hera nodded, "Well said, Master Yenca, well said."

"We have some food and water gourds for Master Domas," said Lemeh, holding them up.

"That was very kind of you masters," said Yenca, "Master Domas, look! More food and water gourds! Let's put them in your robe pockets."

Domas ignored them all completely. "*There in the lake, there in the lake!*" she sang playfully. Lemeh and Hera laughed with delight seeing Domas in her ecstacy and ready to leave for her pilgrimage.

"Come," said Yenca, and pulled Domas to her so that she could put the food bags and gourds into the extra pockets that she had sewn in Domas's robe. "You'll be glad to have these tomorrow. See what it is, Master Domas? See? It's water in the gourds, and food in the bags. Will you remember to eat and drink? It's a long way to the lake. Thank you so much, Masters," she added.

"We are honored that Domas wanted us to come," said Lemeh. "Did she tell you she wanted only us?"

"She was clear about it before she came into her full raving," said Yenca.

"Well, we are very honored," said Lemeh, directing her speech to Domas. But Domas seemed hardly to notice her.

"There in the lake, there in the lake!" Domas repeated.

"Will you take this lantern with you, Master Domas?" asked Yenca. She tried to put Domas's hand around the handle of the lantern, but Domas declined to grip the handle. "Well, maybe you don't need it. The moons are both out, and you can see."

"Yes, it's light enough to see," commented Hera, "It is a good night to depart."

"It is a wonderful night for Master Domas's departure," agreed Lemeh.

"It is your time, Master Domas," said Yenca, patting her kindly on the shoulder, "You may go now. Farewell, dear Master Domas." Yenca tried to look in Domas's eyes, but Domas made no eye contact.

"The time has come, and I am leaving!" she said, and took a few steps away from the gate to the road.

"Farewell, Master Domas!" said Hera.

"Farewell, Master Domas!" said Lemeh.

Domas continued to mumble to herself as she took short clumsy steps away from them and started on the road. The caretaker and the ro-masters gazed after her for a long time, watching her shuffle away. They watched her cross the North Route Bridge and continue far up the road and until she was no longer visible.

Decoration

Alone on a wide stretch of grassland far northwest of the capital, Domas shuffled with tiny, mechanical steps toward the hill country and Lake Ceulan. Her robe, hanging slightly askew over her boney frame, was weighted with heavy pockets full of water gourds and dried food to last her for her journey, but she seemed to have ignored them completely and was marching along with no signs of exhaustion.

The rising morning sun warmed her back as she walked into the wind with her shoulders slumped, muttering to herself as she went. "...*from which gate do I depart, when my pilgrimage I start,* ... name the poet and the context ... *to carry it and its precious content ... carry it and its precious content ...* how does it go? *from which gate do I depart ... ?*"

Her face was speckled and spotted with age, her body bent and thin, but her eye held a rapturous gleam. Over her head was the crisp blue sky of late summer, ahead of her the grassy knolls of the hill country, like a spine on the horizon.

In the inner sanctuary of the Beyanic Temple, Tilke sat cross-legged facing the center of the room. A shaft of light from a window in the roof was slowly crawling with the morning across the floor before her, but she did not stir. She was only a second-generation server, but had advanced in her mastery of the exercises at a pace unprecedented in the temple, and was now very deep into a mind-stilling. She dismissed the awareness of physical sensations one by one as they arose. First the heaviness of body weight, then the odd sensation of floating sideways. Eventually came the peculiar feeling that her limbs and torso were turning into filaments, growing thinner and lighter until she was weightless. Then the strange balance of simultaneous hugeness and weightlessness. This too she dismissed. Then there was no *who-am-I*, no *what-am-I-doing*. No names for, or even sense of whom they called the Soft One.

She was becoming Her.

Simol was just straightening the back of Elenn's green guard's robe and brushing a bit of dust from her broad shoulders, carefully so as not to touch the tender spot on her neck, when Benar ducked under the tarp at the doorway to the Flatpool District guard's station.

"Master Benar!" said Elenn. "You didn't need to come all the way over here — we have to pass by your residence on our way anyhow." The service to honor Master Hela was taking place in the field behind the Quarterhouse compound.

"Well I wanted to make sure your guard's robe was acceptable. How did it turn out? Color all right?" she asked.

"It's perfect, Master Benar," said Elenn, "Thank you so much!"

"Yes, it looks very fine!" said Benar.

"You didn't fall asleep while you were dyeing it this time, eh?" said Simol.

"Master Elenn! You told Master Simol about my little accident?"

"Not without love, Master Benar," said Simol. "Besides, we're all Quarterhouse masters here—no need for secrets."

Elenn couldn't suppress her laughter. "You should have seen her, Master Simol—she was green from head to toe!"

"Oh, but listen to this!" Benar giggled. "Later on at supper, all that the masters could talk about was how the water in the bathhouse had all turned green! Of course I acted as if I knew nothing about it!" They all laughed together at this.

"In any case, thank you for your trouble, Master Benar—you've been very helpful." Elenn knew it was an understatement—there was no way to thank Benar adequately, or any of the masters who had supported Elenn despite the concerns and fears they must have kept to themselves. She felt she owed a debt of gratitude to the whole capital. The best way to pay it, she knew, was to maintain the same attitude required to serve Lern Beyana—one of being pleasantly at peace. It was not something that came naturally to Elenn, but she was learning that she did have the power to choose it.

"It's been my pleasure to work with you, Master Elenn," answered Benar. "And look at you now, about to be recognized for extraordinary service, and it hasn't even been a novade since you left Quarterhouse!"

"How are you doing in here, Masters? Just about ready?" It was Deben ducking under the tarp. "Simol, the visitors from Redrock want to meet you after the services. I told them that you were one of Master Hela's best friends. Of course they're looking forward to talking with you as well, Master Elenn." Deben was focused on the seriousness of the day's tribute to Hela.

"Yes, I'm looking forward to talking with them this evening at the banquet," said Simol, "I hear the Redrock masters like their yeastdrink."

"Yes, it's true," said Elenn. "You can count on that."

"Well then, tonight, we'll be doing some toasting to Master's Hela's memory."

Deben noticed the strap rising from below the collar of Elenn's robe to the back of her neck. It was a covering, she had learned, for the glass tube implanted to direct skullsap from the umbilical artery. The individuals with barren syndrome were having to adjust to being suddenly identifiable for what they were, but so far it seemed to be working well to alleviate their symptoms.

"Master Elenn," she said cautiously, "I see they've replaced your bandage."

"Yes, Master Ferin let me put in the permanent piece a little early since I was going to be taking part in Master Hela's tribute."

"Well you look just fine," said Deben with a spirited nod of encouragement.

"Master Elenn! Who, may I ask, can be given credit for this superb show of calligraphic skill?" Benar was looking at the scroll on the station wall.

"I have no idea," said Elenn. "It looks like work from one of the unnamed, doesn't it?"

"*A uedin's best effort is her purest exercise*,'" read Benar. "I've never heard that before. The calligrapher needed a little practice, but I think the proverb itself is wonderful."

"Master Wanba found that rolled up in the storehouse and had it remounted when I was a trainee," said Deben. "We don't really know where it came from."

"The crude brushwork rather suits the quotation, don't you think?" commented Elenn.

"Yes, I agree," said Benar. "It wouldn't communicate its point if it had been written with a fancy, skilled hand. The more I look at it, the more I get a feeling that the work itself is the result of a very pure exercise indeed."

"Let's go now," Deben said, heading out the door. "All the Quarterhouse masters and unnamed will be assembling soon, and guards are coming from all over the capital."

Simol, Elenn, and Benar followed Deben out of the station, down the road and past a row of blossoming hailflower trees towards Quarterhouse.

END OF BOOK 1

PREVIEW OF BOOK 2

In *Of Guards And Caretakers: Book 2 of the Barren Trilogy*, the story resumes toward the end of the novade, after the younger generation have taken name. Having accepted the medical intervention that allows a barren uedin to live a normal life, Elenn continues to serve the capital as a Flatpools guard. Though she wrestles less with her own internal struggle, she must now negotiate conflicts and dilemmas that arise in interactions with other uedin who are impacted by the growing epidemic. There are very few capital guards who are syndrome-afflicted, and they are called upon to form a special squadron dedicated to addressing the problems that emerge when the medical intervention doesn't work exactly as planned. Elenn and her partner guard will face the challenges together, all the while probing deep questions about cooperation, loyalty, and sympathy. They will furthermore have to contend with the plight and misfortunes of their own lives, deprived of hope for passing-of-life and given only the consolation of companionship.